M[...] of the Lord follow you + lead you always!

Presley

STONES OF REMEMBRANCE

A NOVEL BY JULIE PRESLEY

Copyright © 2012 by Julie Presley

All rights reserved. No part of this book may be reproduced or transmitted in any form or by any means without written permission of the author.

Published by Presley Publishing 1029 N. Saginaw Blvd. Ste F10-229 Saginaw, TX 76179

Scripture taken from the HOLY BIBLE, NEW INTERNATIONAL VERSION®. Copyright © 1973, 1978, 1984 Biblica. Used by permission of Zondervan. All rights reserved.

The "NIV" and "New International Version" trademarks are registered in the United States Patent and Trademark Office by Biblica. Use of either trademark requires the permission of Biblica.

Cover Design: Kyle Steed @ www.kylesteed.com
Photography: Keith Peeler @ www.kpphotoblog.com
Printed in the United States of America
ISBN: 978-0-9859291-0-7
Library of Congress Control Number: 2012914133

Dedicated to my family. Whether it is by blood or spirit that we are related, it is because of you that I am where I am today, and I am so blessed to have this kind of love in my life.

Prologue

Dear Laya,

    First of all, you have to promise not to tell Mom and Dad this. Do you promise? I'm waiting . . . Okay. Good.

    We heard gunshots last night—a lot of them. Like, machine gun shots. I couldn't even tell what direction they were coming from, but I knew they weren't coming from our village. I was terrified. My friend Jenna and I were in the middle of acting out the story of Noah and the Ark for the village kids while our team leader shared his testimony through a translator to the adults. Jenna and I both froze, but the kids didn't even seem fazed. None of them batted an eye. I looked over at our translator, and he, too, was just waiting for us to continue. Jenna and I hurried through finishing the skit, and afterward one of the little girls who has kind of attached herself to me, Subin, came up to me and tugged on my arm. The translator saw her and came over and asked her what she was doing. She told him to tell me that I didn't have to be scared when I heard the sounds of war. She said that the God who protected Noah from the flood would protect us as well. She said that just like Noah sent out birds to find safety, that God would send the birds ahead of us to warn us of danger. I didn't know what to say to her. She, who is brand new to a knowledge that God even exists, just believes so blindly! I pulled her into my arms and hugged her tight, and then I tickled her arms and she squirmed away, giggling.

The translator explained that the people of our village believe that if the war came too close to the village, the birds would take flight in fear, and that would be the sign that the army was heading in our direction. He told me that he'd never heard anyone refer to the birds taking flight as a sign from God until that moment with Subin.

I was speechless as I found my way back to my tent with Jenna. I was still scared. I realized how much more difficult it is to trust in God now than to trust in God when we were kids, when we just soaked up the sun at the lake without a care in the world. We didn't have a clue what was going on anywhere else. But I know now. I am aware now, and I don't think I'll ever be the same.

The people here are so beautiful. They are so kind and generous; they take joy in sharing what little food they have with us. I, of course, feel awful eating it because I know that they don't know where their own next meal will come from, but I can see the joy of sharing in their eyes.

"Take! Eat!" they repeat until we do exactly that. Every time someone feeds me, I try to find a way to sneak some of our own rations of rice and beans back into that person's supply. I got caught once by one of the older women in the village and she yelled at me! I'm not sure if she thought I was stealing or if she was just offended that I would return the hospitality that way, but I've seen her a few times since then and she just glares at me! I have to bite my lips from laughing sometimes when I see her.

I know you're wondering how I'm doing with all the dirt and sanitation issues and I want you to know that I'm actually all right. I have to turn my head away from some things—for example, the community toilet, which is basically just a big hole in the ground. There's no privacy there whatsoever. I am really glad that one of the guys on our team, Jesse, brought a special tent for such purposes. It's a glorified outhouse, but at least it has four walls around it.

Even though I am so encouraged by the people everyday and the Lord is teaching me like crazy, I am so overwhelmed by the epidemic of war and disease that is happening here. We are just a few people trying to make a dent in a place where hundreds of thousands are being attacked all the time. We drilled one well here in this village, but what about the next village over? It seems like the needs will never stop. That's why . . . now, (again) don't tell Mom and Dad. I want to tell them in person . . . I'm not going back to school next year. I'm coming back here to Sudan. I know you're probably freaking out right now, but trust me, I know it's what I'm supposed to do. I want to make a difference here. I want to give my life to these people. It makes that verse really make sense now: "Greater love has no one than this: to lay down one's life for one's friends." These people have become so much more than friends to me. They are family. Subin spends at least an hour a day in my tent, coloring in the coloring books that you sent with me, singing sweet little songs, and playing with my hair. Her mother has really taken to me, as well. The language barrier seems like a nonissue sometimes. It sounds cheesy, but they speak the language of love here and that is a language that doesn't need translation—or words, for that matter.

In spite of all the love I feel here, I really do miss you, Laya! I miss all of you. I hope things are going great for you. I'm sure you're *spending every minute with Matthew, lost in his eyes. Ha, ha, ha. Okay, okay . . . I know, he's Mr. Wonderful, right? I wish I could talk to you, Laya To hear your voice. Living without Internet and a cell phone is brutal! I'll definitely have to figure something out for when I come back, like satellite Internet or something, so that we can Skype! I'm so used to having everything at my fingertips. It's a stark contrast to what these people (and me, now) face every day: Waking up not knowing what the day holds or if that day will be our last.*

Well, I have to go play a round of dodge ball with the kids now. I promised them I would. I miss you like crazy, and I can't wait till next month when I get to see you again!

Love, Marielle

Marielle set down her pencil, folded up the pages she had scripted so carefully to her sister, and sealed them in one of the stamped and addressed envelopes she'd brought from home. A sigh escaped her lips as she thought about the comforts back in America. For the first summer she could remember, she was not with her family at the lake house. She longed to be with them—to sit on the dock and watch the sunset over the blue mountains, to watch the ripples of fish or children jumping in the water. But she knew she could never go back and look at that life the same way again. The impoverished, oppressed children playing just outside her tent had changed her forever. She knew she would never be the same, and when she really thought about it, she knew she didn't want to be that person again. She didn't want to be the self-absorbed girl who was concerned with things that, in the grand scheme of life, really meant nothing. That's why she was planning to go home, sell whatever she had of value, convince her parents she was doing what God wanted—she knew that would be the hardest part—and then return to Africa. Her heart was for the people of this village now. She couldn't stay away. She took another deep breath as the truth about the next chapter of her life settled in her for the thousandth time. There was no use fighting it. God had called her there and all she could do was accept it and give her life to these children.

She tucked the envelope safely into her journal and wondered when she would have the chance to get to town and mail it. She felt her heart lurch as she gazed at the family photograph that was tucked under the window flap of the tent. The sound of children reached her ears, and she pushed all other thoughts from her mind and stepped outside.

The landscape was brown; the sun scorching. Mud huts with wilted straw ceilings were scattered around her, and, in the center of it all, a small group of children were gathering. It was just like the pictures that fascinated her as a child. It was just like she had imagined, and the missionary stories she'd heard so many times at church were completely true.

As soon as the children saw that she'd emerged from her tent, they began calling for her.

"Ma-Ray!" they called in their stuttered accent.

She held her hands over her eyes, shading them against the glare of the sun, and grinned at the kids as a flock of birds scattered overhead.

"I'm coming!" she shouted, even though they couldn't understand her. As she began jogging over to the group of children, a shot rang out. Marielle froze mid-stride, looked frantically this way and that, and then, in a split second, all hell broke loose.

One

The last words her sister ever wrote, scrawled on pieces of tattered and tear-stained paper—having been read and re-read countless times during the past two years—were tucked safely into the suitcase in the trunk of the blue Honda Civic as the little car cruised down the highway. Allaya Sheldon pounded out the rhythm that was pulsing from her stereo as she steered her car away from the city. She didn't know why she was going now, why she was suddenly ready, but last Thursday she had woken with a start and she knew she had to go.

Returning to the family lake house was the one thing she never thought she'd be able to do. Too many memories were buried deep within those walls. Too many family pictures lined the shelves. But there she was, following the highway route that she remembered well from years and years of summers spent at Herron Lake.

She rolled down the window, took a deep breath, cranked the stereo even louder, and gripped the steering wheel, unwilling to allow any emotions or regrets to surface.

"I've got to get to the lake," she whispered under the sound of the driving bass and drum beats.

When she saw the sign announcing that the turnoff for Herron Lake was a mile away, a knot formed in her stomach. She pressed on the gas and sped up. If she could just get there, then maybe the creeping desire to turn around and speed off in the opposite direction would disappear. She just had to get there.

Allaya wiped nervously at her face as she made the turn and slowed down to accommodate the gravel road that led to her destination.

A battered and decrepit sign greeted her from a few hundred feet away: WELCOME TO HERRON LAKE BEACH.

It seemed to scream at her. As if on cue, she felt a stinging in her cheeks as hot streams of tears began to slide down them.

"There's no going back now, Laya," she swore to herself, and she held her breath as she drove past the sign. "There. I did it. I'm here."

She continued to follow the road, catching glimpses of the late August sun dancing on the lake through the trees, passing familiar cabins, playgrounds and hiking trails. It was only minutes before she reached her family's cabin. None of the Sheldons had been there since that horrible summer; that she was the first one to return was a miracle in and of itself.

Parking the car beside the cabin, Allaya opened her door slowly, immediately overwhelmed with the familiar scent of dust and pine. She tried not to put too much thought into anything other than getting her suitcase and the few food staples she'd brought along out of the car. She didn't even look at the cabin until she'd lugged all of her belongings to the wooden stairs. When she did look at it, she did it with a deep breath.

Her heart was immediately overwhelmed with sadness. The deck was clear of everything except a few Adirondack chairs and a small wooden table between them. There were fresh flowers in the window box and the deck had obviously been swept clean. Carolyn's touch.

That was sweet, she thought to herself.

She heaved her suitcase and grocery bags up the stairs and stopped again in front of the door; it was a symbol. Nothing but that solid green door stood between grief and healing. She knew it would be much more complicated than that, but for now, the important part was just to walk through it.

With tears stinging her eyes, Allaya took her hand off her suitcase and placed it on the door, turning the handle slowly. When it started to creak open, she let out the breath she hadn't realized she'd been holding. As familiar smells thick with memories washed over her, she took one step into the kitchen, grabbed the counter directly beside the door for balance, and slumped across it, tears streaming.

After she composed herself, put the food away, and brought in her suitcase, she desperately needed fresh air. Being all alone in that cabin was suffocating. She changed into her swimsuit and sought refuge on the dock as quickly as she could.

Sounds of the past assaulted Allaya's ears while she sat in lonely silence, staring out at the lake. She closed her eyes and remembered. She could see them—three sisters and a lone boy—splashing and dunking each other. She could see the crowds of vacationers resting on the rocky beach, soaking in the sunlight. A sad smile spread across her face as she remembered what life had been like.

Allaya opened her eyes and looked around at the empty beach, at the calm water that lay just beneath her dangling feet. She ached for the days she remembered—the days when her life knew no grief.

"Now or never," she sighed as she slipped off the dock and into the water.

The water's frigid temperature stabbed at her skin as she fought the urge to climb back out and seek warmth in the August sun, so she swam to the bottom quickly and grabbed a small rock from the bed of the lake. Propelling herself upward, she reached the surface and gasped for breath, letting out a shrill screech. The sun was shining strong and the air was hot, but the lake, like any other northwestern body of water, didn't respond to the heat.

Allaya swam over to the dock, pulled herself up, wrapped her towel around her torso, and sat down, turning the rock over in her hands. Just a simple rock to anyone else, but to her it symbolized more than she even cared to acknowledge: endings versus beginnings, open wounds versus healing. She sighed and looked at it thoughtfully, remembering all the hours she had spent with her family in this lake, collecting stones, pebbles and rocks for their garden. It had taken them years, but they had finally collected enough rocks to border their garden and the walkway up to the house back in Portland. The rule had been that everyone got one rock per day, and whatever rock he or she picked up, that was the rock that person had to keep. As if her family were right there with her, she could hear her sisters and her parents arguing about the rule.

"Why can't we just get a whole bunch of rocks at once?" Marielle had asked as she ran her hands across the row of rocks sitting on the sill of the picture window of the lake house.

"Every year!" Shara had groaned and buried her head in a pillow.

Allaya smiled to herself as she remembered the explanation her dad had given at least twice for each week they had spent at the lake:

"Well, Marielle, each of these rocks is like a song," he had explained, animatedly gesturing with his hands. "The good ones stick with you; they play over and over in your head." He picked up a jagged black and white speckled stone. "If one of these rocks has anything special about it, for instance, if you see this rock"— he picked up one of the day's finds— "and you remember this conversation—"

"For the love, Marielle! Remember this conversation!" Shara snorted.

"Then that rock will stick with you," Dad continued. "And when you walk through the garden and see this rock, it will mean something to you. If we had just dived down and dragged a whole bunch of rocks up from the bed of the lake, well, they'd just be a pile of rocks! And of course, then there would be nothing to hold the lake down, and it would just shimmy up into the sky and we'd never be able to come here again."

"Da-ad!" Marielle giggled.

Shara rolled her eyes.

He had been right, though, Allaya reflected. They had scoffed at the tradition, but once the garden and walkway were finished the girls could easily pick out the peculiar rocks that held some memory or meaning.

"Oooh! I remember this one!" Shara had said once. "That was the day that the Meyers's boat sank to the bottom of the lake!" She crouched down to examine the rocks that lined the family's garden back in Portland.

"I remember cutting my hand on this one, and then I had to go to the doctor because the cut got infected. Why we continued to swim in that cesspool after that I will never understand!" Marielle had remembered with a disgusted look on her face as she ran her finger over the scar on her palm.

On the dock, Allaya leaned back on her elbows and lifted her face up so the sun kissed her skin. Her towel unwrapped itself and slid to her sides.

"The good old days," she said quietly to herself, barely aware of a tear slipping down her cheek. She lowered her arms to lay down, focusing on the sound of the water slapping against the dock.

The lake had always been a place of peace for her, a place of refuge. At the end of every school year—in fact, two weeks before—the girls would begin the countdown to the family's departure to Herron Lake. It was there that each of the girls in their own right could escape whatever troubles plagued them at home or at school. Boys, friends, tests, responsibilities—no matter what went on during the year, the lake was a haven, and the girls could breathe easily knowing nothing was required of them.

Allaya reveled in that same peace now. This was the only place where she could escape and truly finish the journey that had been forced upon her two years earlier. This was where she could find herself again, and with it being the end of the summer, she was virtually alone. Most of the families who vacationed here had returned home to prepare their children for the new school year;

there were only days left until it began. Only two or three families remained, and they weren't in the vicinity of Allaya's refuge. The cabins to the left and right of the Sheldon's were within shouting distance and shared the dock, but enough trees and brush surrounded them that privacy wasn't usually an issue. If she wanted company, there was public beach access a mile down the dirt road. But she needed solitude, and she was thankful that she had it.

The sound of a car door slamming brought Allaya out of her relaxed state. Sitting up and squinting her eyes, she turned to see a familiar, beat-up old Chevy down at the next dock. There was Finn Meyers, pulling his bait box and fishing rod out of the bed of the truck. He glanced over at her and, after a minute, he waved. Stunned, she waved back and began to gather her things. It had been years since she'd seen him, and she wasn't prepared for the flood of emotions and memories that coursed through her mind as she saw him and his truck. She took a deep breath and secured her towel around her chest.

"Hey, Ally! I heard you were up here. Wasn't sure if I'd run into you or not," he called out to her. She grabbed the rock, shoved it deep into her bag and started to walk down the dock toward the truck.

"Hi, Finnigan," she called. He hated his full name. She'd often called him by it, having made it her goal to irritate him endlessly. Finn's parents were the owners of the only grocery store in the small town thirty minutes south of Allaya's family's cabin, and they were caretakers for many of the properties on the lake during the off-season. His family had been around for as many years as Allaya's family had owned their cabin. Only Finn's mother remained now, though. Mr. Meyers had passed away from lung cancer when Finn and Allaya were teens. For a few weeks every summer, Finn had become one of the girls' best friends, and, as the years went on, his status changed from friend to crush to non-entity and then back to friend. Each of the three girls had had her secret crush on him, but he was, as were most boys, oblivious. He and Shara were caught kissing once, and that was the first time he'd shown interest for any of the girls. Shara and Finn had been so emotionally scarred by the lectures they'd received, though, that Allaya had wondered if her sister would ever dare kiss another boy again.

Finn rolled his eyes at the sound of his full name.

"So, classes start next week don't they? How long are you here?" He pulled Allaya into an awkward hug.

She froze at his touch. She couldn't remember the last time she'd been hugged.

Pulling away quickly, she fidgeted with the sunscreen in her hand. "Yeah, I'm just here through the weekend, I have to be back at the school on Monday."

"Last minute escape?"

She shrugged and looked the other way. "Something like that. What about you? What are you doing here?"

He gazed at her curiously. "I'm helping my mom take care of the last of the summer merchandise and I'm closing up some of the cabins for the winter. But right now I am going fishing. Would you like to join me?" He pointed to a second rod in the truck bed.

"What?" she looked back at him quickly. "Oh, no thanks. I've already been out here for a while. I should probably get out of the sun."

Finn turned his head to look at the water and said, "Oh,

okay. Maybe another day."

"Have fun, though. I'll see you around," she said dismissively, turning toward the cabin.

"Yeah, I'll see you around," he repeated her words and watched her walk away, lingering a little longer than was polite before turning back to his truck to unload his canoe. Her honey-brown hair radiated in the sunlight, and he had to physically shake his head in order to remember what he had set out to do in the first place. He picked up his whistling where he'd left off, hauled the canoe into the water, grabbed his fishing tackle, and—with a few hopeful glances toward the Sheldon's cabin—he sighed and proceeded to the boat.

TWO

Allaya draped her towel over the porch railing to dry, left her flip-flops at the door, and went inside to shower. She rinsed off whatever the lake had left on her skin, even though she'd barely been in it for a full minute.

Allaya smiled, remembering her youngest sibling's passionate speeches and respect for all things clean and healthy.

"Germs are germs, and they're everywhere! Get in the shower and wash all that grime off," Marielle would have said if she had been there.

Surprising that she was the one who had decided to go to Africa and work with refugees in Sudan, Allaya thought as she lathered her hair with shampoo. She remembered the day that the trip to Sudan had first been broached, and she remembered that Marielle's germ-a-phobic tendencies had come up as well.

"She just wants to make the world a better place by teaching the little African children how to live clean, healthy lives," Shara had teased.

"Daddy, it's a reputable organization," Marielle replied, ignoring Shara's comment. "Sudan has seen so much destruction and warfare, and there are villages where the women and children have to walk for miles just to get clean drinking water, so in order to help them, this team goes in and drills a well for them right in their own village, and then we—"

"We?" her dad interrupted her.

"We, being my team, the missionaries. We go with them and we teach the locals about hygiene and how to care for their children as best as possible given the conditions that they're in. And then, Daddy, we tell them about Jesus! We show them his love. Daddy, please let me go. I want to go so badly!" She was pleading, fluttering her eyelashes at her father.

Terrence and Audrey Sheldon exchanged concerned glances.

"Mom and I will talk about it, Ray-Ray, all right? We'll pray about it, and then we'll decide."

She turned to face her mother. "Mom, please, I know it sounds dangerous, and it is, but I've never wanted to do something and go somewhere so bad in my life. I want to do this. I want to go and share Jesus with these kids. I want to help them live longer, healthier lives."

"Marielle," Audrey replied gently. "You heard your father. We will talk, pray, research a little, and then we will decide."

"When is the deadline?" Terrence asked.

"Two Mondays from now I have to turn in my deposit," Marielle answered.

"You're going to raise all that money?" Audrey looked unconvinced.

"Yes! All $2,500."

And she did. Her parents had released her to go, and she worked her hide off to raise the money to go on the trip. She made calls to friends and family for support; she babysat, dog sat, house sat. No one had ever seen her so excited about anything before. She rallied the youth group at church to donate supplies like toothbrushes and coloring books for the children. There was no doubt that it was Marielle's destiny to go to Sudan.

No one had accounted for the fact that it would be her destiny to die there, as well.

Allaya shook the thoughts out of her head and the water out of her hair. "Okay, Lord," she demanded, "If you want to fix anything in me, or break anything, or whatever—now is your chance. I can't go on like this anymore."

Wrapping a fresh, oversized white towel around her bare body and securing it at her chest, she went and stood in front of the window that overlooked the lake. The sky was full of pink and orange hues as it kissed the sun goodnight before slipping behind the mountains. She could see Finn's boat out in the middle of the lake; it didn't really look like he was fishing but napping, perhaps. It wasn't hard to distinguish his body from the canoe, even at that distance. He'd been scrawny and gangly in the days when they had been busy doing cannon balls off the dock and having water fights, but he'd filled into his tall frame and was well-stocked in all the right places. Allaya could easily make out his torso, which had been stripped of its shirt, and his arms were supporting his head against the bow of the boat. Stretched in that position, she could see the ripples of a six-pack on his stomach.

She'd been so surprised to see him, and she felt guilty for brushing him off—he had been a lifelong friend—but she'd been used to doing that to her family for the past two years. She had more important things on her radar. She hadn't come up here to relive the past, but to deal with it, to put it behind her, and hopefully, to find the footing she needed to step into her future. Her stomach growled, reminding her that it was around dinner time, so she went to the kitchen to unpack a few of the supplies she'd brought with her.

She nuked a bowl of spaghetti that she'd brought from home so as not to waste it, and grabbed her journal off the kitchen counter and retreated to the couch. Settled into the overstuffed flowered cushions, she secured her towel for the hundredth time and glanced around the room, her mind overwhelmed with memories from past trips to the cabin. The whole cabin was decorated in typical woodsy fashion, complete with a mounted deer head, which the girls had affectionately named "Joe," above the fireplace. Her mother's touch was there, too, in the flowered couch and the delicately painted scenes of flower-covered fields and silver lakes. The walls were forest green with brown and burgundy accents, the coffee tables were made of raw wood, and a patchwork quilt covered the back of her father's chair.

She envisioned her father sitting there the last time they'd all been at the cabin together as a family—in his brown leather chair with a cup of coffee, his reading glasses, and his old, worn Bible. She thought of her mother humming in the kitchen, fixing cold cuts and rolls for dinner. She imagined Shara in the bedroom the three sisters shared, pouting about being whisked away from all forms of media, entertainment or social life, and about being forced to spend what she called a boring week at the lake. Marielle was, well . . . she was . . .

"Gone," she said out loud. A tear slipped down her cheek.

Finn lay with his back to the sun, thoughtfully considering all that his short conversation with Ally had afforded him. He thought about his initial reaction when he saw her on the dock; it had felt as though there had been a sock in his throat. Her once-sparkling blue eyes seemed almost gray, and dark circles shadowed them. It had shocked him to see Allaya seem so detached and dismal when the girl he remembered had always been so full of mischief and playfulness. There had always been some kind of secret dancing in her eyes, but now it seemed that someone had stolen her secret and told the whole world. There was no mistaking the grief, and it pained him to see that she was still suffering so deeply over the loss of her sister. How does one reconcile herself to such a loss?

It was a terrible blow when his mother had called him to tell him about Marielle. He'd collapsed onto the nearest chair, and then, after hanging up, he stumbled into the bathroom and threw up.

Finn knew that it had taken time for notification to reach her family. Marielle had left for Africa with a group from her college that worked with a water drilling company in Sudan. The group had been there for only two weeks when their camp was raided; there had been very few survivors. Most of the American team had been killed as they attempted to defend themselves. Many had been wounded, including Marielle. Apparently, she had suffered a stab wound to the abdomen, which under the circumstances quickly became gangrenous and infected. The wounded waited desperately for some kind of help, some kind of miracle. The medical supplies had been torched in the raid, and there was little food for nourishment. Their vehicle had also been destroyed in the raid, which made the journey to the nearest town a full day's walk each way. Even if they could reach a town, there would have been no assurances that the right supplies would have been available, or that they would even have been received as friends and not as enemies. The two brave village men who decided to take their chances at finding help were never seen or heard from again, and Marielle suffered for three days before she passed. It took another week just to get word to her family, as communication travels slowly without Ethernet cables and telephone lines. Just days before Marielle's scheduled flight home, the family received the news. The few that survived the wait were eventually rescued after one of the refugees escaped from the militant army and ran to the nearest village for help, bringing back another team of Americans with him.

    That was really all Finn knew. He had grieved for his friend and her family, and he had attended the memorial service with his mom nearly two years ago. He could see that the entire Sheldon family was shell-shocked by the loss; Allaya in particular seemed catatonic. Suddenly the family that he'd grown to love as his own for a few months every year appeared before him as strangers. Mrs. Sheldon squeezed his hands while tears ran down her cheeks. In the receiving line, Mr. Sheldon, no longer caring about that stolen kiss from the past, patted Finn's shoulder and gave him a strong hug.

    "I'm so sorry, Mr. Sheldon. I don't . . . I just can't even imagine," Finn had said.

    He felt stupid, like any words he said would only drive the nail further into the coffin, so to speak, and that he should have said nothing at all. Mr. Sheldon's eyes welled up and he merely nodded his head. Finn had simply hugged both Shara and Allaya. He wasn't even sure that Allaya had recognized him, or for that matter, anyone else at the service. That had been the last time he'd seen any of the Sheldons.

Finn shifted his gaze from the scenic view and looked toward the cabin where Allaya was now. He had no idea how she had fared in the months, and now years, following Marielle's death. All communication between them had stopped; from what he knew, Allaya had pretty much shut herself off from the rest of the world.

He didn't know why he had felt the need to come when his mother asked for his help closing up the cabins. His mother had never needed any help before, and his need to be there really had nothing to do with her at all. He couldn't explain to his on-again-off-again girlfriend Tanya why he had to leave all of a sudden. He had come to the point with her where he really didn't care how she felt about anything—he could never do anything to please her, and he was weary of trying. He had called his few clients and told them that their carpentry projects would be delayed a few days, but that he would take good care of them for their patience. He loved heading to the lake for quiet, to get away from that whole American Dream thing, but he had never felt the need to be there like he did now. His mom had let him know that Allaya was going to be there, but Allaya didn't seem like she wanted any company or like she needed him at all.

"So help me," he said aloud, shaking his head. "If she even trips, I'll be there to catch her." His words surprised him as much as they comforted him. For some reason, the pit in his stomach, the one that started growing the moment he had seen her on the dock, was creating a feeling of responsibility within him.

He sat in his boat in the middle of the lake and stared thoughtfully at the cabin for quite some time.

Allaya stretched out on the couch, staring at the blank page in her journal. It was starting to wear not from use, but from the fact that she had sat with pen in hand, staring at that page, almost daily for the last two years. The previous page held the last entry that she had written before the news was delivered that her little sister was dead.

Oh. My. Gosh!!! I think I'm getting married!!! I mean, no, it wasn't a proposal, but . . . he wants me. I don't know if anyone has ever wanted me like that. Marielle is gonna freak. I can't wait till she gets home next week. Not being able to talk to her this month has been torture. Ugh! I wish it were next Tuesday!!! I miss her!!! I can't believe that for the first time ever, I'm in love, and I can't even talk to her about it! This is killing me!

Maybe I'll torture her with my secret before I let her in on it. That'll teach her to run off to Africa! Wow. He loves me. This is amazing. I have this crazy feeling in my chest.

That was it. It was so insignificant in the wake of what came next. How was she supposed to know, though, that it would be her last entry, that it should be meaningful? She had been so self-involved, though she did wonder about Marielle's safety and prayed for her every day. Still, self-gratification had been her focus.

Looking up from the journal, she prayed, "Here I am, Jesus. I am where you asked me to be. For the first time in a long time, I am listening and I want to obey. I don't know how you are going to fix this, I wish you could just erase . . . No, I don't wish that at all. Ugh!" she grunted and put her face in her hands. "Jesus, I need you."

She left it at that. There was nothing else to say. She didn't expect an instant change or lightning bolts or anything like that, but almost immediately, it started pouring rain outside. Allaya gasped and ran to the window, too distracted to care that her towel had come untucked and had dropped to the floor. She pressed her hands and her face against the window as lightning shot across the sky.

"Oh my gosh," she whispered.

Storms at the lake were the most glorious storms ever. From the big picture window that overlooked the shimmering body of water, she listened and watched as the rain pelted the ground, the thunder declared its ownership of the sky, and the lightning cut through the darkness like a knife, illuminating the water that rippled with every raindrop that fell.

Ever since they were children, Marielle and Allaya had been enamored by storms at the lake. They could always be found curled up beside the picture window, fast asleep the morning after a late-night storm. Allaya had often thought thunder was the sound of God's heart breaking—a bittersweet beauty. She stood watching, mesmerized for an hour, completely lost in the moment and in the silent words that spoke to her heart. She didn't notice the tears streaming down her face. All she was aware of was the feeling that something was being ripped off her heart like a Band-Aid.

Three

He didn't mean to see her or to stand in the rain staring up at her. Finn had just pulled his boat back to the dock as the rain started coming down in sheets. He looked up at the sky and was distracted by the illuminated window and the movement in it. He would have done a double take, except that his first take never had the chance to recover.

Did she know she was naked? Never mind that. Stop looking! he scolded himself. But he stared at her. She never saw him, and for as long as she stood there, completely vulnerable in the window, he stood, barely remembering to breathe, staring at her.

As the storm eventually quieted to rain, she stepped back from the window and his trance was broken. He ran a hand through his hair, looking around as if to see if anyone else had witnessed what he had witnessed, and then remembered that he was alone on the lake. Suddenly he was aware of the pouring rain, that he was soaking wet, and that he had a 30-minute drive ahead of him back to town.

What in the hell is wrong with you? he thought.

He started for his truck, but was struck by the thought that Mr. Sheldon probably had some clothes in the cabin.

Dry clothes that could replace his rain-soaked clothes.

But if he ventured up to the house would she know that he'd violated her private moment? Could he cover up whatever it was that was rising like a blaze within him? That thing, along with the image of her that had been seared into his brain, was unnerving. He wasn't a pervert; it wasn't his fault she'd been standing there naked in the window for anyone to see.

You didn't have to stare, he reminded himself.

"Yeah," he sighed. "I did."

He leaned against his truck and lifted his head to the sky, letting the rain continue to soak him and hoping it would wash away the image and cause the fire inside him to fizzle and burn out.

Finn knew he wasn't perfect. He lived his life the way that felt right to him—he didn't take advantage of anyone, he wasn't cocky or proud. He was an all-around good guy. He knew that he had to overcome the natural desire inside himself. He'd seen naked women before, and he knew what it was to make love. Regrettably, he also knew what it was simply to have sex and that the former was definitely the more desirable. He knew that the Sheldons were "believers" and that Allaya hadn't stood in the window like that to tempt him or lure him. Even still, he was a man. There had been a time when he had thought about God but he'd never had any experiences worth writing home about, so he'd lived by morals he felt were fair. He thought he'd done well up until he'd seen Allaya, but nothing could have prepared him for his response to that angel in the window.

Tanya who? he thought to himself.

His desire confused him. It wasn't just that he was aroused—because, yes, he was—but it was that he had an insane longing to be with Allaya. To know her. To help her put the pieces of her life back together. There was an invisible force that was pulling him to her.

It won't hurt to just see if some of Mr. Sheldon's clothes are there. I won't stay long, he reasoned with himself as he turned away from the truck and walked the short path to the cabin.

Allaya had secured the towel around herself again and had moved from the window to the floor where she was again trying to tackle the empty page of her journal. She jumped from where she sat at the sound of the rapping on the door. She searched frantically for a blanket to cover her towel-wrapped body. Seeing her robe on a chair in the kitchen, she grabbed it, and, after leaving the towel on the table, wrapped the robe around herself.

"What in the world?" she muttered. She tiptoed over to the window to peek out just as Finn shrugged and turned to start walking back down the stairs. Flinging the door open, she called out to him.

"Finn! Oh my gosh! You're drenched! Come in! Come in! What are you doing out in this storm?"

He dropped his head. "I got caught on the lake," he lied. "I just got the boat tied up, and I thought maybe your dad had some old clothes left here? Dry clothes? The heat in the truck is out and—" He was fidgeting, and he felt like a fool.

"Oh! I'm sure there are! Here!" She grabbed her towel off the table and handed it to him, shutting the door behind him.

Wow. So not helping, he thought. The scent of her shampoo lingered on the towel and his clothes as he dried off. He squeezed some of the water from his hair and clothes, took a deep breath and smiled sheepishly at her.

"Thanks."

"Follow me." She led the way down the hall to the master bedroom and yanked on the closet door.

"It gets stuck sometimes." She grunted and finally got the stubborn door open. He turned around pretending to look around the room, but in actuality, he was trying to avoid staring at her.

"Hasn't changed a bit," he murmured, looking around the room.

The woodsy theme extended throughout the entire cabin. The master bedroom had dark green and blue wallpaper with a mallard duck border around the ceiling.

"Here we go. They might be a bit big, but they'll get you home! I'll just uh . . . go . . . change," she said as she started out the door.

"Oh, no, you don't have to do that," his eyes grew large in embarrassment. "I mean, I'll get out of your way right after I get these on."

"Your mother would kill me—my mother would kill me—if she knew I let you go back out in this rain without letting you warm up first! You'd just get soaked all over again and have to come back for more clothes!" She smiled softly.

"I'll make some decaf," she said and walked out the door.

He slumped against the closed door and dropped his shoulders, groaning on the inside. He didn't dare pick up that towel again; it was dripping with the scent of her shampoo. He dressed quickly and went into the living room. Noticing the pile of wood beside the fireplace and at the same moment how chilly the house was, he got to work. By the time Allaya emerged, he had a small fire blazing.

"Thanks. You didn't have to do that," she said as she and Finn walked back into the kitchen. "Do you like cream and sugar?"

"Uh, yeah, a little of both."

He felt like a schoolboy. His palms were sweaty. He was nervous, tongue-tied. She had put on a green hooded sweatshirt and old pair of sweats, but she was beautiful regardless.

Why is this just occurring to me now? He tried to shake the strange feeling that was making him feel like a teenager again. *I have known this girl for most of my life. I have seen her a thousand times!* He shook his head, trying to clear his mind. *But then again, I've never seen her naked before tonight.*

"You okay?" She was staring at him with a mug outstretched.

"Oh! Uh, yeah . . . water! Um, in my ears." He wanted to slap himself. Instead he reached for the mug, careful that their fingers not touch, lest he self-combust.

If she noticed how ridiculous he was acting, she didn't let on. She sat down with her mug and looked at him.

"I'm sorry about this afternoon. I was rude to you."

"Don't worry about it, Ally. I didn't mean to intrude on you," he shrugged.

"No. You didn't! I just . . . ugh." She shook her head and continued, "I'm just not in a good . . . well . . . you know."

She leaned her face on her right hand; her other hand rested on the table and toyed with the handle of the mug.

"Yeah." He didn't know what to say and so he busied himself by taking a sip of his coffee, fiercely controlling his facial expression when the heat singed the taste buds on his tongue

"Well, enough about me," she said dryly, "what is going on with you, Finnigan?"

"Will you ever stop doing that?" he grimaced.

Allaya gave him a small smile and shrugged. "Still doing the carpenter thing?"

"Yeah, still doing that."

"Pays the bills?"

"Yup."

"Dating?" she asked cautiously.

"No—er, well . . ." he stumbled, not sure what to answer. He couldn't even conjure up an image of Tanya's face.

"Aaaaah, one of those," she smiled.

"What do you mean, one of those?" he asked as she cocked an eyebrow and looked at him sideways. "Okay, fine, yes, one of those," he relented. "So, to answer your question. No, not right now."

"Tell me about her."

"Why?"

She shrugged again, "Take my mind off of other things."

"I could think of a lot more interesting things to talk about."

"I'm listening," she said playfully.

"Huh? Oh! Uh . . . um, world peace, for example. The problem with the environment. Squirrels."

That brought a smile to her face and he caught his breath.

"If she's that horrible, why are you with her?" Allaya probed.

"I'm not with her," he said quickly, "and, I don't know. I really don't. I mean, she drives me crazy. She's always nit-picking and complaining. I guess sometimes there are no better options out there, and being with someone is better than being alone."

"See, now I much prefer to be alone these days, if you couldn't tell," she rolled her eyes.

"Is that a hint?"

"Hmm? What? No!" Her cheeks flushed. "I'm sorry, Finn. I didn't mean it like that."

He chuckled, "It's okay. I'm teasing, sort of. Really though, I'm still in Seattle, still doing woodwork, doing a lot actually for some of the ocean-front community in Oregon. I've managed to do pretty well for myself. I've got a good life. I'm happy," he took a drink of his tea and quickly added, "for the most part." He looked at her expectantly. "Now your turn. You don't have to talk if you don't want to, but it's been years since I've seen you or heard from you and—." he trailed off, fearing that she would shut him out.

"I know," she took a deep breath. "I'm sorry, Finn."

"You don't have to apologize, Ally." He touched her hand. She stiffened but she didn't move. He cleared his throat, looked intently at her and carefully removed his hand.

"Please do not apologize, Ally. I mean, it's not like we were life-long friends or anything—"

She gave him a pained look. "We were, too!"

"We still are," he smiled at her softly. She shifted her gaze to the table and Finn straightened up, unsure if she was uncomfortable, too.

"Well, I've pretty much been in survival mode for the past two years. After Marielle died and Matthew ditched out—"

"Matthew?"

"Oh, yeah," she sighed, shaking her head. "Matthew. This guy I was seeing. It was getting pretty serious. We were talking about getting married, being in love, all that," she waved it off. "Well, it took me weeks to even get out of bed after the funeral, and I guess he got bored or impatient or something, and I wasn't responding to anyone, so he left," she shrugged. "He said he was sorry, but he didn't know what to do to help me and that he didn't know how much longer he could wait it out. I was pretty miserable."

"Ass," Finn stated.

"Well . . . yeah, I guess, but I don't really blame him. I mean, what was he supposed to do? He would have ended up leaving eventually. What guy in his right mind would put up with this for two years?" she motioned to herself. "So, anyway, he left, and eventually I had to go back to work. It was torture trying to function like a normal person every day."

She turned her mug slowly in her hands, catching herself, once again trying to push the hard memories to the back of her mind.

"You okay?" Finn asked after a quiet moment.

"It's just hard looking back," she shrugged.

Finn nodded, looking back was something he wasn't a fan of either. "I think the rain stopped," he said quietly.

"Oh? All right. Well, you can just bring those clothes back whenever." She took their mugs to the sink, dumped them out and then rinsed them. He wasn't about to let her off the hook that easily.

"Or, I could bring them back tomorrow around lunch and we could go for a hike?" he offered with eyebrows raised.

She eyed him warily. The day had been emotionally draining on her as it was, and she really didn't know if she could handle being social.

"I don't know," she started.

"An hour, tops, I swear. I'll bring lunch." His eyes were soft but piercingly green, like emeralds. She sighed and studied his face for a moment. His unkempt brown hair, in need of a trim, was falling across his eyes and was still a bit stringy from the rain. His cheeks were well defined and when he smiled, his entire face reacted to the movement: laugh lines formed under his eyes and on his forehead. She considered his offer: *What am I really going to do all day alone? An hour. I can handle an hour. This is why I'm here anyway. To re-enter the world, and make peace with its inhabitants.*

"Sure. A hike sounds good," she said with a nod.

Once in his truck and safely out of earshot, Finn groaned and let his head fall to the steering wheel.

"Is this a cruel joke?" he asked the darkness. He started the truck, cranked the radio and tried to get the image of Ally standing naked in the window out of his head. He had to get a grip on himself. A grip on the thudding in his chest.

You absolutely 100 percent cannot get close to her tomorrow.

He'd never had a problem keeping his hands to himself, but the feelings growing inside of him were causing him to doubt that he had any self-control at all. He hadn't wanted to leave the cabin. He would have sat with her all night in silence if she'd let him. He would have been content just to be in the same four walls as she was. That was a lie. He would have managed to be in the same four walls as Allaya, but he would have been fighting the urge to pull her to him in the hopes that he could kiss her in a way that would make her forget all about her pain.

Laying in bed that night, Allaya was surprised by her anticipation of the next day's hike. It had been good to spend some time with Finn. She hadn't meant to divulge anything about her process, but if there had been anyone to share it with, Finn was the safest. He always had been. Safe and genuine. It was easy to feel comfortable with him, to feel like herself. That was new. At home and at work, she felt like she was wearing someone else's skin. She was a stranger even to herself most days.

Not tonight, she thought. *Maybe this is it. The beginning of change. My metamorphosis.* She knew she could not return to the person she had been prior to Marielle's death, but whoever she had become afterward needed to change. Life would continue to drag on without any hope or joy if she kept holding onto her pain. But letting go could be painful, as well. Pain had become her companion, her excuse and her security. She wasn't sure what "Allaya" would look like on the other side of letting go. There was so much uncertainty, so much trepidation. But the two things she knew for sure were that now was the time and she would not walk the path alone. That much had been promised by the Father when she had made the decision to obey the nudge she'd felt to come to the lake, and seek healing.

She sighed, pulled the blankets up around her chin and rolled over, willing herself to sleep.

Four

Finn woke up far too early. The sun shone brightly through the window as it crept up over the mountains. The earth seemed at peace with the sky once again after the loud, wet clash they'd had the previous night. Finn looked at the clock, groaned, rolled over, and pulled his pillow over his head. That was a lost cause. He was not going to be able to go back to sleep. Turning over again, he focused his eyes on the ceiling, again trying to talk himself off the proverbial ledge of his crazy, unbiased, and inexplicable attraction for one of his oldest friends. He'd known Allaya for most of his life, and nothing had necessarily changed about her . . . but that wasn't really true. Everything had changed about her, and given the current state she was in, he knew there was no way she would entertain the idea of him pursuing her.

Back off, fool, he thought to himself.

He felt discouraged all morning as he made attempts to distract himself from the clock. He busied himself around the store, and he even tried to convince himself to call Allaya and cancel their plans. His cell phone vibrated in his pocket as he collapsed boxes in the back room of the store.

"Tanya," he sighed when he saw the caller ID show up. He flipped the phone open and instantly regretted it.

"Hey, Tanya," he answered.

"Finn! Finn, I tried to call you all day and all night last night!" Tanya sounded frantic.

Precisely why I left the phone at home, he thought while wandering back to his bedroom.

"You did? Oh, hmmm. I must have left my phone here at the house," he said.

She groaned. "I hate it when you do that! I was worried about you! Are you coming back today? You know it's Andrew's birthday tonight; we're supposed to be there."

"Yeah, yeah, I know, but I'm not gonna make it back in today. My mom still needs my help getting things taken care of here," he said, "and one of my old friends is here and I kinda want to catch up."

"Oh," she said, sounding hurt. "Is he from college?"

"Uh . . . no," his voice going up an octave. "Just an old family friend."

He didn't feel the need to tell her that the friend wasn't in fact a he, but rather a wounded and captivatingly beautiful she.

"Anyway, I need to run—" he trailed off.

"Fine. Whatever," she said in a huff. "I'll just see if Jesse wants to go with me."

He could hear that she was trying to get a reaction from him. Jesse was a guy she worked with who had been pursuing Tanya for months. There had been many fights with Finn about the amount of time she spent with him, even while they were not technically dating. It had gone almost as far as a fistfight one night when Jesse followed them to a bar and got in Finn's face.

He rolled his eyes.

"That's a good idea. Have fun!" He flipped the phone shut and stifled a laugh.

He could just picture the look on her face on the other end of the line. They had broken up for what seemed like the thousandth time a few weeks prior to his trip to the lake, and, for the first time, he found that he didn't really care what she was going to do or whom she was going to be with. He hoped his response just then helped her to know that. He knew that she would bring up Jesse in order to manipulate him, and usually she'd eventually wear him down to get what she wanted. But maybe the clean country air—or maybe the knot growing in his stomach whenever he thought of Allaya—had changed things for him. Tanya and Jesse were the least of his concerns. He felt a need, a responsibility, for Allaya that he'd never experienced before. He shook his head at himself.

She doesn't need you to save her, he thought, trying to convince himself.

His frustration began to slip away as he realized there was only an hour left until he was to pick Allaya up for their hike.

Looking into the mirror from across his bed, he sighed, "You're an idiot," and left the bedroom.

His mother was in the kitchen, still in her men's-style pajamas, her graying hair pulled back in a ponytail. She was packing the lunch that Finn had requested the night before. She'd put on a little weight since the last time he'd seen her, but she had always been so slight of frame, the extra pounds were good for her. Otherwise, she seemed the same as she always had, at peace and in control.

"Sweetheart," his mother greeted him as he walked over to kiss her on the cheek.

"Thanks for doing this, Mom."

"Anything for the prodigal son," she said with a wink.

"Ha, ha, ha. Very funny. Let's see, what do we have here?" He peeked in the bag.

"Two turkey and Swiss bagels, two bags of chips, two apples, and two granola bars. Enough?"

"Sounds good."

"Finn."

"Yes'm?"

"Go easy on her," she said, looking up at him with concern.

"What do you mean? We're not going far, and the hike isn't uphill or anything. It's just that trail out on the north end of the lake. We've been out there hundreds of times!" he sputtered.

"Honey," she said, smiling softly and reaching a hand up to his stubbly face, "that's not what I meant."

He tilted his head and questioned her. The knot in his stomach twitched.

"She is still damaged, and you just need to be patient. Go easy, and take it slowly with her."

"Mom! I—"

She interrupted him. "Babe, I knew you were coming here before you knew you were coming here. I know what is going on inside your head and in that stubborn heart of yours." She placed a hand over his heart and gazed up at him lovingly. Finn turned his eyes down and ran a hand through his hair. He grasped the island, leaned over and hung his head as his mother rubbed his back in encouragement.

"I don't know where this came from! I mean, how do you even . . . okay, I know where it came from, but it's . . . well, it's insane! I mean, I've known her my entire life almost, and now this happens? Now it hits me? Ugh!" He sunk his face into his hands. "And damaged? That doesn't even begin to describe it! I mean, we all have problems, but come on, her sister died. She is still so, so . . ." He fumbled for the right words.

"Broken?" his mother pitched in.

"Yes." He slumped against the counter even further.

"You can't fix that, you know."

"I know. I want to though. I would give anything to see some life in her eyes again. It's . . . it's painful to see her like this. It seems like there's a dark shadow hanging over her head."

"Oh, sweetie," she said as she rubbed his back affectionately. "That pain may never go away. She will heal, and she will be able to face life with hope and happiness again, but there will always be pain in the place where Marielle should be." She wiped the corner of her eye. "You just don't get over that kind of thing. But Finn, she will be able to deal with it eventually, and right now, she just needs you to be there while she figures out how."

"But mom, I don't know if . . ."

"You can. You can help get her through it, and then you'll see. You can wait."

He stood a little taller and said quietly, "I was not expecting this."

Carolyn Meyers put her hands around her son's face and turned him to look at her. "Expectations can cause failure; they can let you down. It's the surprise that gives you excitement and hope. She is your surprise." Her eyes, glistening with tears, held promise and wisdom. But it was lost on Finn.

"Oh, brother. Is that followed by 'thus sayeth the Lord?'" he joked as he pulled away from her grasp. But she tightened her grip.

"Finn, I'm not telling you what to do or trying to take control of your life. All I'm saying is that you have to take it easy."

"Geez, Mom, it's only been a day! I'm just . . . just . . . rebounding!" Fighting for words, he managed to slink away from her grip. He grabbed the backpack, a few water bottles from the mudroom and took them out to the truck. He pulled his hiking boots out from the cab and crouched down to lace them up. Finn stood up and found his mother standing in front of him. He leaned over and kissed her cheek.

"Thanks for lunch," he said.

"Finn, just take it easy," she reminded him.

"Mmhmm, yup. Got it." Rolling his eyes, he climbed into the truck, roared it to life and drove off onto the main highway toward the lake.

Carolyn watched the truck disappear over the hill and prayed silently: *Father, please give him patience. Continue to chip away at the walls of Allaya's heart, prepare her for whatever it is that you are doing here. And Lord? About Finn . . . yeah . . . you know.* She sighed and turned to walk back inside, checking the water level on her flowerpot by the door.

"Oh!" she yelped when she stood up and peered through the window into the laundry room. Mr. Sheldon's clothes lay folded neatly on the dryer. She had completely forgotten to give them to Finn.

Finn drummed his fingers on the steering wheel as he drove. His phone had rung twice since he'd left his mom. The first call had been Tanya; he'd quickly hit the ignore button. And the second had been his mother letting him know about the clothes.

"So if you don't totally lose control today, you'll have another reason to see her again," he said as he looked at himself in the rearview mirror. Something on the side of the road caught his eye in the reflection of the mirror. He slowly pulled a U-turn on the deserted road and headed back a few meters.

Passersby might consider it odd to see a man on the side of the road standing over a fallen tree, looking at it intently, dragging it to his truck—struggling alone to hoist it up into the bed. But this was his livelihood. He was already envisioning the pieces of furniture he would create from this casualty of nature.

He wiped the sweat from his forehead, closed the tailgate and patted the tree. The exertion of dragging the fallen tree to his truck had helped calm his nerves; he felt more in control of himself. Maybe that log would prove to be just the distraction he needed. With a deep sigh of accomplishment, Finn turned the truck back toward the lake.

"Gosh! I haven't been out here in years!" Allaya exclaimed as she took in the beauty of the woods. The sound of their footsteps crunching on leaves was soothing to her ears as Finn led her down a familiar path through the trees.

Soft green moss covered the ground on both sides of the

trail. Berry bushes speckled the landscape, and tall pines and spruce trees towered over them as they crunched down the trail. There was a slight breeze, which carried the scent of the previous night's storm, and the branches swayed back and forth in it, as though the wind had asked them to dance and they'd been delighted to accept.

She stopped to breathe in the pure fresh air, feeling strengthened in the familiar setting. She loved being so far removed from the city life, and from the pressures of it, even in spite of the reasons why she had chosen to remove herself so briefly. There was nothing for her to do at the lake except bask in the calm. The pain in her heart seemed dulled in the bright light of the sun and the warm breeze that rustled the leaves and needles on the trees. One side of the trail sloped slowly upwards as the mountain began its ascent skyward. The other was more uneven, covered with random boulders and pine trees, and completed with a view of the lake, not twenty feet in the distance.

Finn hadn't realized she'd stopped and he was trucking ahead on the path. He turned around to say something and saw her a number of paces back, eyes closed and head tilted up toward the trees, leaning one knee against a boulder with one knee up for support. The few rays of sunlight that reached through the swaying bows of the trees danced across her face.

There's that angelic thing again, he thought as he swallowed a lump in his throat.

He had kept it cool, kept his distance. Conversation was at a minimum. His mother was right; he needed to be patient. It was unlikely she would accept an advance from him ever, much less if he just pounced on her without warning. The whole thing still had him reeling. He wasn't sure what he wanted. Her hair was almost honey colored in the sun, and his gut was in knots again, just like the previous night. He wanted to slap himself. He needed a distraction. He looked at his watch. They'd been hiking for just twenty minutes, but he'd promised her only an hour.

"Are you ready to eat?" he asked as she straightened up to catch up to him.

"Hmmm?" She looked up at him, startled.

"I, uh, I asked if you were hungry."

"I could eat," she said, shrugging her shoulders, but he saw something flicker in her eyes.

"You all right?" He took a few steps back toward her.

She smiled distractedly. "Yeah, I'm fine, I was just remembering something."

"Care to share?"

Her cheeks pinked a little and she smiled. "Remember when Marielle and I snuck some of your dad's cigarettes?"

He grinned and answered, "I don't think I'll ever forget how ridiculous the two of you looked blowing on a couple of Marlboro's."

Finn's throat closed again as the smile crept slowly up from the corners of her mouth and spread to her eyes. He could tell that those eyes hadn't reflected a smile like that in a long time and that they needed to, desperately.

"I can't imagine how much more ridiculous we would have looked if we'd figured it out and had actually sucked on them. I would have hacked up a lung! And I did when I finally inhaled one in college." She stepped toward him.

"I miss those days," he said softly.

"Are we eating?" she asked, turning away from him.

"Yeah, Let's see." He looked around for somewhere to

sit. A huge rock sat by itself to the left of the path.

"That looks like a good spot." He started toward it and Allaya followed a few steps behind. Just as Finn reached the rock, he turned to see Allaya trip and land face first in the ground.

"UMMMPH!"

"Ally!" he shouted as he ran back to her to help her up. "Are you okay?"

She brushed the dirt from her shorts and hands and laughed nervously.

"Ugh. Yes. Just embarrassed," she said as she looked up at him. "Do I have dirt on my face?"

He snickered and reached a hand up to brush the dirt from her forehead and nose.

"Just here. And here." Her skin felt clammy with perspiration, but soft and smooth. He quickly pulled his hand away.

"Are you sure you're not hurt?" he asked, taking a step backwards.

"I think I'm all right," she said. But she took a step forward and faltered, squealing in pain. "Crap. I twisted my ankle."

"Here, take my arm." He couldn't avoid touching her now. He just tried to keep her at arms length.

So much for keepin' my hands to myself, he thought.

"Do I smell?" she asked as they hobbled over to the rock.

"Do you smell? What?"

"For a crutch, you're awfully far away!" she looked at the ground while she hopped on one foot.

"Well, I didn't want to say anything, but—" he joked, but he took one step closer to her as they reached the rock. He helped her up and then sat down beside her, feeling frustrated with himself.

He struggled with where to position himself, not wanting to sit too close or too far to give any one impression. He was having to use far too much brainpower trying to keep in line with good intentions. He tried to relax as he pulled their lunches out of his bag, and then he helped her prop her foot up on top of the bag.

"Compliments of my mother," he said as he handed her a sandwich. He noticed another smudge of dirt right above her lip and chuckled.

"You have a mustache!" He grinned down at her.

"What? Oh!" She reached up to wipe her mouth but totally missed the spot.

"Here, hold still." He took a sharp breath and reached forward to wipe the dirt from her face. It would have been so easy to pull her face toward him and kiss her lips, but he quickly pulled away.

They ate in silence at first, listening to the frogs and the crickets, the wind and the birds.

Then she spoke: "I hate the city."

Finn cocked his head to one side in question, "What?"

"Shhh. Listen."

He glanced around with his eyebrows raised and his head still.

"What am I listening for?" he asked.

"This!" She waved her arm and gazed at their surroundings. "I am so sick of the sirens and the honking and the motorcycles and all the other stuff that happens outside of my apartment window. It's all ugly, man-made, no, man-ruined!" she exclaimed. "Everything you hear out here is God-breathed. None of it is fabricated or trite or touched by humanity. This is pure life." She took another bite.

Finn stared at her quietly for a few seconds. "I suppose you're right. I grew up here, so sometimes the quiet is like a jail sentence for me. Sometimes I just want to know that there is still life beyond these trees. But I remember during college feeling the way you do now. I would use this place as an escape from all the racket. It took some getting used to, living in the city, but I don't mind it now."

"We are so different, you and I," Allaya said thoughtfully. "I suppose that's why we work."

"We work?" he questioned, his pulse quickening.

"Yeah, I mean, despite a few years in our adolescence, we've always gotten along really well, don't you think?"

He drew in a breath. "Yes."

"Opposites attract."

He chuckled at the double entendre, of which she was obviously unaware.

"Mmmhmmm." He focused his attention on his sandwich.

Allaya looked around thoughtfully at their surroundings again. "I think I remember this place. I know I've been out here hundreds of times but isn't this home base?"

Finn looked at her questioningly and asked, "Home base?"

"You don't remember?" she gave him an incredulous look.

"Uh . . ."

"Capture the Flag?"

She saw it cross his face the minute he remembered, and together they both said in unison, announcer-like voices, "Capture the Flag, The Ultimate Showdown." She gave a small laugh and he threw his head back.

"Wow. I'd completely forgotten about that," he said.

"We were a good team," she said thoughtfully.

"It wasn't exactly a fair game though," he laughed.

"Oh, I know. We tried to make it even! Marielle had such a crush on that Aidan kid, and he and his brother were terrible runners, but she didn't care, she wanted him on her team."

"It wasn't about the game for her." He smiled as he remembered Marielle's face swooning over the thirteen-year-old boy whose family had visited the lake that particular summer.

They both fell into a comfortable silence until Finn perked up.

"Home base," he muttered, crawling over the huge rock the two were sitting on. "You're right! This is it!"

"Huh?"

"Can you scoot over here?" He reached his hand out to help her and she shifted carefully over the rock and hung over the edge of it.

"No way. I totally forgot about that!" she sighed as she saw the words **Finn and Ally, CTF Ultimate Showdown Champions Forever!** scrawled in black Sharpie on the huge rock.

"Wow," she whispered.

"We dominated that game."

"Why did we call it the Ultimate Showdown? There wasn't anything ultimate about it!" She shook her head.

"That was the time we had those big plans to play in the

dark with flashlights and the Anderson kids were going to come, too, but then their grandma died and our parents nixed the flashlight thing."

"Oh yeah," she sighed and traced her fingers across their names.

"I can't believe it hasn't been washed away by rain or anything," Finn said helping her back up to a sitting position.

"Some things don't wash away," Allaya said wistfully.

"Ally . . ." He was relieved when she interrupted him. He wasn't sure what would have come out of his mouth if she hadn't.

"Don't, Finn. Please." She shook her head and bit into her sandwich. She'd had enough remembering for the time being, and she knew that whatever Finn felt like he needed to say to her would push buttons she wasn't willing to deal with yet. He had already unknowingly uncovered a depth of emotion in her that was surprising and unsettling.

He nodded silently and looked out over the lake. They finished their meals in quiet and packed up, careful to clean up all their trash.

"Are you going to be able to walk back?" He helped her stand up.

"I'll manage."

"Are you sure?"

"I'm fine, Finn," she said curtly.

"All right," he shrugged and helped her back to the path and then let go of her hand, ready to lunge forward if she fell again.

FIVE

This is ridiculous, Allaya thought as she took a step forward, away from the steadying grip of Finn's hands. She winced and stumbled. She didn't have time to turn and admit defeat before Finn came up from behind her and took her arm again.

"You're not fine," he said as he guided her back to the rock. He gave her the backpack and swung her up onto his back, piggyback style. Her pride was wounded, but she was surprisingly at ease with her friend whisking her back to safety. She smiled a little as she imagined him as her knight in shining armor, though a little less glamorous without the trusty white steed. She imagined what she must look like, a grown adult riding on another's back, and she suddenly became aware of his hands on her legs. Her breath caught in her throat and she shifted against him.

His fingers loosened on her calves slightly and he turned his head back: "You all right up there?" he called.

"Mmmhmm," she said quietly, and then, trying to diffuse

the nervousness that had suddenly pitted itself in her stomach, she added with a chuckle, "Giddy up!"

"Um, what was that? You want me to drop you?"

"Still can't take a joke, Finnigan?" She was amazed at how easily her personality had raised itself from the dead in the past twenty-four hours. Maybe God did know what he was doing after all; at least he seemed to this time.

As for Finn, he felt he couldn't have been put in a worse situation. Well, he supposed he could have, but he refused to even imagine those possibilities. He'd tried to keep his distance from her, to control the desire burning inside of him to press his lips against hers, to trace his fingers around the long slope of her neck as she looked away from him, but now he had actually become the savior he'd convinced himself she didn't need.

When they reached the cabin, he helped her up the stairs and into the house, leaving the door open behind them. She hobbled with his help to the couch and sat down. Finn grabbed some throw pillows and propped her foot up on them.

"Ice packs?" he asked as he headed to the kitchen and closed the front door.

"No, but there is ice in the freezer and there are sandwich bags above the microwave," she called after him. He took his time filling the bag with ice, leaning on the counter for a few minutes, breathing deeply and thinking that maybe he should get himself some ice as well.

Allaya was resting her head against the armrest, facing the back of the couch. Her leg hurt much worse than a twisted ankle. It was more likely sprained.

Great. Now I am cooped up here, not that I was going anywhere else, she thought. She hoped that Finn wouldn't feel obligated to stay. His mom needed his help, and he didn't need to be distracted by her clumsiness.

Allaya swatted mindlessly at a buzzing behind her head. "Shoo, Fly." she said, and then she felt a sharp pinch on her neck. "OUCH!" she cried and jumped up from the couch, forgetting about her injured foot.

Her ankle buckled under the pressure and she fell over, catching herself on the coffee table. Finn came rushing out, once again, just in time to see her falling. She landed with one leg straight out, one hand balancing herself on the coffee table, and the other hand rubbing furiously at her neck.

"What happened?" He ran to her side and grabbed her elbow.

"I think I got stung by a bee," she whined.

She slumped onto the couch and Finn pulled her hand away from the area she was rubbing on her neck, leaning in to get a closer look. His breath was hot on her neck and sent chills down her spine. She shuddered.

"Yeah, it's a bee sting. The stinger is still in there. Do you have tweezers?" he asked, just inches from her face.

"Yes, in the bathroom. I just used them this morning; they should be on the counter."

He leapt up and disappeared around the corner. Sitting rigid, she tried to make sense of the thoughts tumbling around in her head. She just needed a moment alone, but she wouldn't get it.

"Found 'em," he said as he returned. "I looked in the medicine cabinet for some allergy medicine too, just in case." He gave her a Dixie cup of water, the box of medicine, and sat down beside her, carefully tilting her head away from him so he could get a good look at the stinger.

"Are you cold?" he asked.

"No. Why?"

"You have goose bumps."

"Your fingers are cold." She mumbled and shuddered at the same time.

"Oh, sorry."

She didn't respond. She could feel tears pricking her eyelids. She blinked quickly, not sure if her emotion was from pain, embarrassment, or something else altogether.

His hand was shaking slightly as he pursed his lips together and aimed the tweezers at the stinger. Allaya had never been one to attract much drama, but in the matter of a few hours she had sprained her ankle and then she had been stung by a pesky bee. And there he was, acting as her savior, exactly what he had been trying to avoid for the last fifteen hours. He was in over his head. This had never happened to him before.

"Got it!" He heaved a huge sigh of relief as he pulled the tweezers back and examined the stinger. Allaya tilted her head back and turned to look at it with him, their faces inches apart. He heard her take a sharp breath. The stinger wasn't that ferocious.

She felt herself wanting to lean closer to him.

Am I nuts? she battled within herself. Everything in her brain told her to sit back, move over, and kick him out, except for this small part that seemed to be louder than the rest of her— her heart thudding in her chest.

He looked up at her, very aware that she had not moved away, that her face was still less than a hand's width from his. Another opportunity to kiss her that he'd have to resist. He gazed into her chocolate-brown eyes and when she didn't break his gaze, he knew he was headed for disaster.

"Ice!" He jumped up quickly and grabbed the ice bag that he had dropped when he found her balancing on one foot.

Allaya sat back on the couch, letting out the breath she had been holding, her eyes wide as she stared at the coffee table, willing her insides to calm themselves. She took a few deep breaths, and ran her fingers behind her neck. Finn came back and sat beside her again, and she was certain he could feel her pulse through the cushions.

He took an ice cube and held it against the red bump that was forming on her neck. He could hardly keep his focus as he watched droplets of water slip off of his wrist and drip down her back, making a dark spot on the ribbing of her black tank top. He rolled his eyes at himself. The scene playing out in his head would destroy any real chance he had with Allaya—if there was one at all—should he act on it.

"Here, you hold this one," he said, gesturing for her to take the cube on her neck, and he moved to the other end of the couch and pulled her leg up onto his lap to inspect and ice it. "This is swelling pretty bad," he said.

"I know. I can feel it. It hurts."

"Do you want to take something for it?" He started to stand.

"No, it's okay. The ice is enough." She put a hand up to stop him. He leaned back, staring at the ceiling, both hands supporting the ice around her foot.

"I'm sorry Finn," she said softly, and Finn's head shot back up in surprise.

"Sorry? Sorry for what?" He raised his eyebrows.

"Sorry that I'm a klutz!"

He laughed at her and said, "Don't worry about it. It's not every day I get to rescue a pretty girl!" He smiled at her and saw something cross her face, pain probably. "Are you sure you don't want some painkillers?" he asked.

Allaya yawned. "No, I'm fine. I think the allergy medicine—" she yawned again— "is going to knock me out anyway." She shifted herself further down on the couch and turned onto her side. Finn adjusted the pillows between her feet, placed the ice on her ankle, and shimmied out from underneath the weight of her legs.

"All right, you get some rest," he said and started toward the door.

"Don't go."

He turned around and quietly asked, "What?"

Allaya mumbled something unintelligible and he walked back over to the couch, not sure what to do. He didn't want to leave her, but at the same time, he didn't know how much more he could take. He leaned over her back and brushed a strand of hair off her forehead and jumped a little when she sighed.

"Ally," he whispered.

Nothing.

"Ally," he whispered again, "do you want me to stay?"

"Mmmmm."

He sat back on his legs and ran his hand through his hair and sighed. The red bump on her neck, though still bulging, wasn't swelling any more. He traced his fingers down the side of her face, her neck and around the sting. He bent down and kissed the red spot gently. There were those goose bumps again. Finn looked around the room for a blanket, grabbed a plaid fleece one from the rocker and covered her up. He brushed her hair from her face again and stepped back. He sat down in the lounge chair, directly across from the couch, and watched the rise and fall of her shoulders as she fell deeper into slumber.

This is insane, he thought to himself. Has this feeling always been here, just waiting to be uncovered? He let his mind wander to summers past, when he and the Sheldon girls had ruled the lake. Thousands of memories flooded his mind, most of them playful and fun. One day in particular stood out in his mind when Allaya had shown him just what she was made of.

"Finnigan Meyers, you let go of her right now!" Allaya had cried out, marching down the dock. Finn looked up at her devilishly from where he held a fighting Marielle, fully clothed, just over top of the water.

"Are you sure?" he grinned.

"Let her go or I'll go get my dad!" Ally stomped.

"Okay, if you say so," he sang and released his grip on Marielle, dropping her into the lake.

"Noooo!" Marielle cried out as her body hit the water with a huge splash.

Allaya froze, wide-eyed. "Finn!" she cried out and then charged him, shoving him with all her might. He flew over the top of Marielle's head and landed in the water right next to her, arms flailing in shock. Allaya bent down to give Marielle a hand out of the water, but Finn shot forward and grabbed it, yanking her in.

She was furious for about the first thirty seconds, but then she dove under the water with her feet barely hitting the surface and kicked splashes of water into his face. Marielle swam over and climbed onto his shoulders, trying to push him under the water, but he easily threw her off. Their war continued until they were all exhausted from battling with one another and they sat laughing on the dock side by side, kicking their feet above the water until their parents came looking for them.

From his position on the lounge chair, watching Allaya sleep, Finn thought hard about those moments, searching for any memory of an attraction or a fleeting thought about her, but he found nothing—nothing but a sense of belonging, playfulness and nostalgia. He sighed quietly as he gazed at her breathing in and out, peacefully on the couch.

"How did this happen?" he whispered.

Six

Allaya was groggy when she woke up; she had always hated the dizzy, medicated feeling she got from allergy or cold medicines. She forgot that she'd hurt her ankle and turned over with such force that she winced in pain. She propped herself up on her elbows and looked around, waiting for the room to stop spinning. She was covered with a blanket, and the ice pack was gone from under her foot. She looked to see if it had slipped onto the floor. Then she heard a clanging in the kitchen.

Startled, she called out, "Hello?"

Finn came out of the kitchen. "Sorry, I dropped a pan."

"What are you still doing here?" she asked, perplexed.

"You asked me to stay," he said, surprised and wondering if he'd read into her request.

"I did? I don't remember." She lay back down and rubbed her eyes. "What time is it?"

"Four thirty," he answered. He looked down. "Do you want me to go now?"

"Four thirty? You wasted your whole day here!"

"I don't mind. I mean, I wasn't bored. I kept busy." In truth, he had sat and watched her sleep for a full thirty minutes before remembering that he had a new project in the back of his truck. He spent an hour sawing off branches with the tools he always carried in his vehicles. Then he had come inside, looking for inspiration for something he could scrape together for dinner for he and Allaya.

"I'm, uh, making you dinner," he said slowly.

"You don't have to do that!" she said as she shook her head, sitting up again. "Really, you don't."

"Allaya, relax! You're hurt and you can barely walk. I don't mind. I have nowhere else I need to be right now."

"What about the store and your mom?"

"My mom will be fine. The store will still be there when I get back." He turned on his heel and walked back into the kitchen. More clanging.

His insistence unnerved her and she was annoyed. Annoyed that she'd gotten hurt—not once, but twice—annoyed that he'd stayed, annoyed that she'd apparently asked him to, annoyed that he was annoying her so much. Mostly, she was annoyed that he was affecting her so much. She fell back into the couch. He continued to clang around and, after about fifteen minutes, emerged with two steaming bowls of chili. He pulled the coffee table closer to the couch and helped Allaya readjust herself so she could eat. She took a bite, begrudgingly.

"How is it?" he asked.

"Fine," she snapped. The sudden cold shoulder surprised him.

"Are you all right?" he asked quietly.

"Yes, Finn. I am fine. Will you please stop asking me that?" she charged. He quietly put down his fork and looked directly at her.

"I think I'm gonna go," he said, picking up his bowl and starting for the kitchen.

She flung herself back against the couch with a sigh. Tears pricked her eyelids. She squeezed them tightly.

Call him back.

It took her a moment to recognize the voice that she had come to the lake to seek out. The one that spoke not audibly, but rather the one that impressed upon her in a way that made her heart pound and her hands shake. Why was God speaking about this though? Why was Finn's presence important? She decided that she didn't care enough to find out.

No.

Call him back.

Why?

Call him back.

"Uuuugh!" she moaned, not loud enough for Finn to hear.

"Finn!" she called. There was no response. *Oh well, I'm too late. He's gone.*

No, he's not.

She shook her head and groaned.

What good can possibly come of this? I can't deal with this right now. This is so not why I am here, she thought.

Silence. Finn had heard her, but he'd already heeded one of her requests that day, and apparently it had been the wrong choice, judging by how upset she had been upon finding him there after she'd woken up. He had carried her out of the woods, nursed her bee sting, made her dinner, and she hadn't even said thank you. It was his turn to be annoyed. He was frustrated that he'd let his mind run away with a stupid childlike fantasy.

I'm acting like a teenage girl, he told himself. Maybe what he'd felt had been nothing but physical attraction. There really was no reason why he should stay. He could find other ways to satisfy attraction. Even with his hand on the door though, something gave him pause.

"Finn?" he heard her call again, this time a little more desperate. He gritted his teeth and walked back to the entrance to the living room. She was wiping the back of her hand under her eye.

"What?" he sighed.

"I'm sorry."

"It's fine," he said. He shook his head and looked away. "I'll see you later, Ally," he started to turn back to the door.

"Finn, come on. I'm sorry. I'm a bitch." She squeezed her eyes tight again. "I don't know how to relate anymore, and I'm frustrated . . . at me, not you."

He crossed his arms and looked at her expectantly.

"Why?" he asked.

"Well, for starters, this," she said, motioning to her foot, "was not how I planned on spending this week. I haven't had much social interaction in a while, and here you are wasting your time on me. I can't just be here at the lake. I can't just exist and enjoy it," her voice started to falter and crack. "I'm annoyed that I'm even here, I mean, that I had to come here, to get away from everything in my life just

to . . . to . . . to get everything back." She sniffed and blinked away hot tears.

Finn's stance relaxed and the anger that had crept in was dissipating. He felt like an idiot. He knew exactly why she was there. His mother had warned him of exactly this mistake; getting emotionally and physically involved with Allaya was a bad idea. His mother had said that Allaya simply needed him to be there. He wasn't sure what he should do. He remained in the doorway and watched her continue to fall apart.

She went on, "I have spent the last two years of my life completely isolating myself from everyone and everything. You know, I have a cell phone, and it rings exactly three times a week. A week, Finn! And it's my mom every time! No one else has a reason to call me anymore because I've pushed everyone so far out of my life. I avoided people, and now . . . now they avoid me!" she sobbed. "Finn, she was my best friend. She was the only person in the world that ever deserved that title! She was my sister, for God's sake. What am I supposed to do? How can I just let go of her existence? I don't even know who I am without her! It's ridiculous! Like we were conjoined or something, and I just can't get over it. I can't let her go. She was my best friend!" She buried her head in her hands and Finn, no longer concerned with her rude behavior, rushed to the couch, though he was at a complete loss as to how to comfort her.

"Ally, I know. I'm so sorry. I'm so sorry." He gathered her in his arms and spoke into her hair. He knew there was nothing he could say or do to relieve any of her pain. It was a hopeless effort, but he had to try anyway. He held her while she cried; he kissed her hair, the top of her head. His heart ached for her, for her family, for the sister and daughter who would never return, but he knew that his ache was no comparison for the depth of Allaya's.

She let him hold her, not completely surprised by her emotional outburst. She'd become very predictable in the past two years, and though there was very rarely any drama to push her to her limits, the slightest infraction would send her into emotional disarray. She heard his words, she felt his embrace, and she felt comfort. Safety.

She cried harder as she realized that she was making a connection with Finn—the type of connection that she had avoided with anyone since they'd found out about Marielle, since the day that she'd found her autopilot switch and had completely shut herself down to the outside world. That switch had been flipped again, and she was awakening to the need she had for human interaction—the one she was ignoring. She'd been surviving solely on fumes, and barely. It felt like she had ripped open a surgical wound in her heart, and that it was bleeding profusely. Finn handed her a tissue and she mopped up her cheeks, pulling away slowly from his embrace.

"I'm sorry, Finn," she whispered.

"Will you please stop apologizing? You've been apologizing for two days. I don't care, Ally. I was being selfish. I'm the one who should be saying sorry."

She looked at him questioningly. "Selfish?"

"Never mind. You can verbally abuse me all you want; I won't take offense. I promise."

She snorted and rolled her glistening eyes. "Thanks, that makes me feel so much better."

He grinned at her. "Do you have any wine?"

"Oh, my gosh. Yes! That is exactly what I need," she sighed and started to get up, again forgetting about her injury. Finn caught her just as she was about to meet the coffee table a second time.

"Hold on there, Miss Independent!"

He was holding her again, though this time they were standing and she wasn't crying anymore. She laughed nervously.

"I'm beginning to think I can't function without you," she trailed off.

"Well, if I hadn't been here, you wouldn't have sprained your ankle," he reasoned.

"I'm glad you're here though," she said softly. "I wasn't at first, but I am now."

Finn's heart thudded to a stop and he released his grip on her. "Uh, where'd you say the wine was?"

"Bottom cupboard beside the fridge."

He was already around the corner.

Allaya's heart was racing. Finn suddenly presented as a huge distraction. Something had changed significantly in the past fifteen minutes. Maybe that wasn't such a bad thing, but she was even more confused than ever. She'd come there to heal, and while she could feel something happening deep inside those wounds, there was something else happening deep inside of her as well, and Finn was the reason.

He returned, one bottle of wine and two glasses richer. She was leaning against the couch with her hand over her face. He resisted the urge to ask her if she was okay, not wanting to annoy her further. Sitting on the far end of the couch, he poured their wine and watched her. Nothing about that day had squelched his thirst for her.

"Thanks." She slid back to a seat on the couch and curled her fingers around the glass he held out to her.

"So," he started.

"So," she said back.

"Why did you come all the way up here?" he ventured, wondering how much she would be willing to divulge about her process. She'd already surprised him with her outburst.

She took a deep breath. "It was time. I knew it was time to deal with this. I knew that God was telling me it was time."

"I get that, but why here? Why the lake?"

"I think I always knew that I would come here to say . . . goodbye," she stammered. "This place holds my very best family memories. This is where Marielle and I became more than sisters. This is where we became friends. Shara, well, you know Shara," she chuckled and gave him a sideways glance. "Yeah, you know Shara—"

Finn groaned. "Gimme a break! That was like, twelve years ago!"

"Yeah, mmhmm!" she teased. It felt good to put the focus on someone else, to tease and to smile.

"Oh brother, Ally. Seriously. We were children. Both of us had never kissed anyone before and we wanted to know what it was like. That's it." Defending himself against such an old and childish transgression seemed silly, but still he felt the need.

"Whoa, Finnigan!" She was surprised at his response. She had no idea that she'd become the object of his desire. She playfully hit his arm. "Lighten up, dude! Here. This'll help." She tipped her glass to her lips and leaned against the couch, propping her foot on the coffee table.

He chuckled and then followed suit, sipping his wine and propping his feet.

She continued, "Well, Shara never really liked being up here—she never hung out with us—so Marielle and I hung out together, when we weren't with you." She paused and glanced up at him. He had seemingly recovered from his offense and was listening intently.

"We were close," she went on. "It was a bit different at home, but we were still close, and every year we got closer and closer. We were best friends, and we had this house, this lake, these woods to thank for it." She paused and closed her eyes, taking a deep, calming breath. "So, when I thought about how I was going to work on this," she said, her finger gesturing to her chest, "I just pictured myself here." She shrugged. "I pictured myself staring out that window, grabbing stones from that lake, crying on this couch. I did not account for a sprained ankle or a bee sting." She took a sip of her wine and swirled the glass and then added quietly, "or you."

There was a moment of silence. If anyone else had been in the room, there would have been no denying what was happening. But the two of them, alone with their own befuddled thoughts, were too consumed to see the other's responses to the force that was pulling their hearts toward one another.

"I remember how much your family loved this place, even Shara," he said. "I think she was just lonely." He shrugged and sank further into the couch. "Why haven't the rest of your family been up here since?"

"I guess it's too hard. I don't know. I honestly don't talk to them a whole lot or on any personal level. Believe it or not, besides my students, you have had more face time with me in the past few days than anyone else in the past two years."

"Wow." He drew in a breath. "Well, I feel honored, that's for sure."

"You should. You are kind of relentless, though."

"Who? Me?" he grinned. "Maybe if you acted like you wanted me around, I'd actually leave, and then you wouldn't have to wish me away!"

Allaya reached to put her hand on his and squeezed it.

"I don't want you to leave, Finn. I'm grateful that you have been here for me. It's just been pretty emotional being here, facing the facts. This is really hard. I mean, you have to keep in mind, again, that I haven't been around 'people,'" she quoted with her fingers, "in a long time. I'm a little rusty."

Finn tapped his fingers together and her hand slid to his arm, practically burning his flesh with electricity.

"Socially awkward, huh? You always were, just a little." He grinned when she rolled her eyes. He took the last gulp of his wine and then timidly took her hand in his own. "So I'm breaking you in, huh?"

"I guess you could say that," she shrugged. Maybe that was what it was about. If that was all, then she could handle that. But it sure felt like a lot more than that. They were quiet for a few minutes.

"Gosh, I'm so sorry that I fell apart on you." She took her hand from his and smoothed her hair back.

"Let's make a deal." Finn scooted toward her.

"What's that?"

"You stop apologizing, and I'll just give you the benefit of the doubt. You're okay, and I won't ask anymore."

"Ha! All right. Deal. I'm not sorry anymore," she smirked.

"Good. You shouldn't be. Lord knows if anyone has a right to have a breakdown, it's you."

"A breakdown?" she scoffed.

"Calm down, it was a joke. Well, sort of," he grinned.

"Ah, so you can make fun of me, but not vice versa?" she eyed him suspiciously and he shrugged and winked at her, sitting back thoughtfully.

"So, do you think you're making progress?" he asked.

She sighed and thought about her answer. "I'm feeling things again, if that means anything," she said, avoiding his gaze.

"I think it does," he said quietly, staring deep into his glass.

"I do, too. It's intense pain, but in that there is a strange sense of peace."

Not quite the feelings he was hoping for.

"I know that I have to do this. I know that I have to let her go, in a sense. She'll always be in my heart, but I know that I can't carry this burden around on my shoulders forever. She would want me to live my life. She would want me to have friends and be close to my family again. Those thoughts didn't even occur to me until last Thursday when I decided to come up here."

"Thursday? You only decided last week?" he was trying to mask his surprise.

"Yeah, why?"

He stuttered, "Uh, no reason. That's, um, just not much time to plan a trip!"

"Yeah, when I called your mom she said she had just been to the house and done a good cleaning, and that it was ready whenever I wanted to come out, so here I am." She sipped her wine. "It was a spur of the moment thing, and like you said, summer is over next week. I haven't done any prep work for classes or anything. This became my priority, which is insane because I've been avoiding it for two years! All of a sudden, like I said, I just knew it was time, and I felt like I was ready."

"Hmmm," he muttered. He sat back, considering the fact that his mom had called him on Monday and asked him to come. He had never understood the inner workings of his mother. She was a mystery to him.

"The storm last night was kind of the ripping-of-the-band-aid, so to speak," she continued. Finn shifted uncomfortably in his seat. If she'd known he'd seen her, she would have said something by now.

"What do you mean?"

"Well, it was so weird. I had just finished praying, asking God to get on with it, and you know, I didn't really expect anything to happen, but almost instantly there was a huge clap of thunder and it started pouring. I was so shocked by the whole thing. This wasn't long before you got here. I actually, well . . . I was so caught up in the beauty of the moment . . ." she trailed off. Her cheeks flushed. "It was so beautiful—it was as if nothing had ever changed, like she was still here." She gazed out the window. "Geez, I'm glad the Morgans aren't here!" The Morgans owned the home next door. "They'd have gotten a good show last night!" she chuckled out loud. "I mean, uh, because I was such a wreck and all, standing in the window for so long like I was paralyzed or something," she covered.

Finn was nearly beside himself. He shifted his weight around on the couch.

"Be right back." He jumped up and walked calmly to the bathroom down the hall and locked himself in, slumping against the door.

There I go, acting like a teenager again, he thought to himself for what felt like the tenth time that day. He pressed his hands against his scalp and tried to get a grip. After relieving himself, he splashed some cold water on his face and took a deep breath, pushing the image of the nude beauty in the window from his mind.

He returned to the couch, looking a little distraught. Allaya took note of the change in his demeanor, but let it slide for the time being.

"Sorry," he said very evenly. She tilted her head, looking at him oddly, but went on.

"Anyway, our favorite things about the lake were the storms and that window right there. We would sit for hours watching the lightning and listening to the thunder and rain. We made up stories to the rhythm of the raindrops on the roof." She rested her head in her hand. "It totally caught me off guard last night, and I just gave in to the pain. I let myself feel it; I let myself bathe in it. Shortly after that, you knocked on the door, more waterlogged than that old tree at the bottom of the lake!"

"Dashing, aren't I?" he teased.

She sighed and rested her head on the back of the couch.

"I expected to be alone up here. I didn't count on you showing up. I figured I would just lock myself away, like I have for the last two years, which, in retrospect, doesn't really make any sense if that is the habit I'm trying to break. But here you are, and here I am, opening up. I am glad you're here, Finnigan, despite recent evidence to the contrary. I'm glad you're here," she smiled.

Allaya turned her head to look at him. She wondered if she was being too open, too honest. But it felt freeing. She had spent so many months locked inside herself, not willing to reconcile anything going on inside of her, ignoring the tapping on her heart, the voice in her head that kept calling her name, softly, and not demanding.

"Ally," he interrupted her thoughts. "Ally, I . . ." he stammered.

"What is it?" she asked.

He chickened out. "It's getting late. I should probably head home." He recalled his mother's admonition for patience. He stood up and grabbed their plates and wine glasses.

She knew there was something wrong, and she tried to reason her way out of it: *I'm attaching myself to the first person I open up to. This is nothing but a mere connection, or reconnection, with an old friend. That's all it is. He's 'breaking me in,' just like he said. That's all.*

This time she remembered her injured foot and stayed put on the couch, planning out her journey to her bedroom, how she was going to bathe, and how she would accomplish her other nightly rituals.

"How's the sting?" Finn asked, coming back into the room.

"It's fine. I barely feel it." She rubbed her hand over the spot on her neck.

"Do you want me to help you do anything?" he asked, a little uncertain how the night would end. "I rinsed the bowls and the glasses."

"You know, I think I'm just gonna sleep here on the couch tonight. I'm gonna put on a really girly movie and cry my eyes out a bit and pass out, right here. I'm not even gonna brush my teeth." She seemed proud of her decision in spite of the thought that crossed her mind: Marielle would have been mortified and would have lectured her on oral hygiene rules.

"I'm definitely leaving," Finn chuckled and she rolled her eyes at him. "All right, well, is there anything you need?"

"Yes. Can you pull down the third disc up there for me?" Allaya pointed to the shelf above the TV with a small selection of movies on it.

"Seriously? Isn't this the one where Meg Ryan and Tom Hanks email each other back and forth?" he laughed.

"I need a good girly movie where no one dies in the end," she replied with a weak smile.

He nodded silently and slid the disc into the DVD player.

"Come here. I need you to do one more thing." She stood and gestured to him.

He walked over to her and she steadied himself on his arm. She pulled him closer to her and wrapped her arms around his neck.

"Thank you," she whispered into his ear.

Her breath was warm against his skin. Chills travelled down his spine as her breasts pressed against him and his hands encircled her waist, the skin of her midriff hot against his fingers. Holding her tight, it was all he could do not to put his lips on hers. She held on longer than was normal, and he knew he could only handle so much.

"Allaya," he whispered, unmoving.

"What is it, Finn?"

"I just want you to know," he paused, his lips brushing ever so slightly against her ear as he spoke, "I'm not going anywhere."

Her stomach fluttered. A warmth spread through her arms and legs and she pulled back to look long and hard into his eyes. In that moment, she knew. She knew they were fighting the same battle, and that he was as equally surprised by it as she was. Her breath caught in her throat and she buried her head in his chest quickly, lest she make a move toward his lips that she might regret.

"Finn," she whispered. She was scared, and she hadn't felt scared in a very long time.

"I'm not going anywhere," he said again over the top of her head.

She nodded against his hard chest. He wanted more than anything to tilt her chin up and kiss her. How many times had he envisioned doing that in the few hours he'd spent with her?

He knew now that she wouldn't resist him. He had seen the look on her face as she searched his.

Patience.

Please! Please let me have this, he begged the voice inside his head.

Patience.

He sighed and released his embrace, turned around and headed for the door.

"Oh!" He suddenly remembered her dad's clothes and turned back to look at Allaya. "I forgot to grab the clothes this morning. Is it all right if I bring them by tomorrow?"

"That's fine. Could you do me a favor?"

"Anything."

"Would you mind bringing me some crutches from the pharmacy back with you?" she asked with a grimace.

"Ally, do you need to go to the doctor?"

"Finnigan, you promised . . ."

"Seriously, Allaya."

"They are going to tell me to elevate it, put ice on it and

use crutches. There is nothing they can do, I swear."

He relented. "Okay. I will bring you some crutches and an ace bandage. I'll be here in the morning."

Her heart pounded in her chest.

"Sounds good," she smiled. Silenty she wished he would stay with her.

He turned quickly and walked out the door.

She collapsed onto the couch. "Holy crap," she said out loud. She never turned the movie on, but sat for hours replaying the events of the day in her mind, and seeing them from a new perspective. "Is this really what you had in mind? This is really how you want me to 'jump back in?'" she asked the empty room, lifting her face to the ceiling. "Just when I think I know what you're trying to do . . ."

Even with all the turmoil inside her heart and her mind, Allaya slept more peacefully than she had in years, for a few hours at least.

Seven

Carolyn Meyers, now dressed in everyday jeans and a button-down top, was lost in thought, drying dishes at the kitchen sink. With an ear tuned to the bell that rang whenever anyone walked into the store attached to her house, she had been praying all day. That wasn't unusual for her, but she didn't always pray with such purpose. The dream she had had earlier the previous week had been so vivid. She knew that the only way she could make any kind of difference in her son's actions was by praying fervently that the Lord's voice would not be lost on him, that he would recognize the need to keep himself in check, and that he would give Allaya all the time and space she needed. She knew the Lord needed to finish the healing process he had begun in both of them.

"I'm home," Finn called out.

Carolyn let out a breath and walked to the mudroom.

"Hi sweetie." She took him by the shoulders and reached up to kiss his cheek. There were days when she still couldn't believe that her scrawny little boy had left home and grown into a handsome adult, no longer dependent on her for much of anything. She'd always wondered where his choices would take him and was thankful he'd not traveled too far away. Now he was back, and even though he didn't know it, she knew that he was on a divine path, one that could go so many different directions simply based on how he dealt with certain situations. The mom in her was desperate for details, but she wasn't going to pry. He was a grown man; she knew he'd talk to her if he wanted her input.

Be realistic, Carolyn, she thought to herself. *He probably won't.*

Finn hung up his backpack and his shoes hit the wall with a thud as he kicked them off.

"Well?" he asked.

"Well, what?"

"Well, aren't you going to ask?"

"Ask what, dear?" She spun on her heel and returned to the sink, avoiding eye contact with him.

"Mom," he scowled, "you know what."

"Finn, if you want to talk about it, I would love to hear. But I'm not going to push you. I told you that."

Eyes narrowed, he watched her as she picked up the damp cloth and started wiping down a plate. "Well, I didn't do anything stupid. Not really."

She raised her eyebrows and cocked her head toward him. "Not really?"

"Well, no, not really. I mean, she tripped and sprained her ankle on our hike, so I had to carry her—well, piggyback her—to the cabin."

"She sprained her ankle? Is she all right?"

"Yeah, she's fine. She was pretty embarrassed by it, though, and she got a little snippy with me."

"Well, good. Someone needs to put you in your place once in a while! It's a heavy load for this mama to carry!" She winked.

"Yeah, well, she also got stung by a bee when we got back to the house, so, with that and her ankle, I stayed to make sure she was all set."

"Sounds like an eventful day." Carolyn placed the last plate in the dish rack.

Finn left out the moments he and Ally shared in close contact, the shivers she had sent down his spine on more than one occasion, and he most certainly did not say a word about when she hugged him and how the closeness of her body against his had nearly been his ruin.

"So, that's all?" she pressed.

"Pretty much," he shrugged. "We had some dinner, she talked about Marielle a bit . . . actually, I guess a lot, considering . . ."

Carolyn looked up at him, her jaw gaping. "She talked to you about Marielle?"

"Um . . . yeah?"

"Oh, Finn! Oh, wow!" She leaned back against the counter and clutched her hand to her chest.

"I know it's a big deal. I guess she's been pretty isolated from her family lately."

"Finn!" Carolyn held up her hand for effect. "It's a huge deal. You have no idea! She hasn't talked to anyone about it. Not her parents, not Shara, not a therapist!" Her eyes were glistening with tears. "She has avoided any chance that Marielle's name might even be mentioned. Audrey said that she only took one call from them a month, even though they call her twice every week. When I told her that Allaya had called me, Audrey started crying on the phone!" She wiped at her eyes. "Oh Finn, this is beyond huge!"

"Well, she said she just knew it was time," he shrugged. "She said she knew that God was telling her it was time to deal with it."

"But Finn, the fact that she felt that, acted on it, and is now talking about it? That is a miracle. Her family has been waiting two years for this. What did you say to her?"

"Mom, I didn't say anything! It was when she got upset with me because I stayed while she was sleeping."

Carolyn narrowed her eyes at her son.

Finn explained about the bee sting and the Benadryl and threw his hands up in defense.

"I was going to leave and then she apologized and that was when she just kind of let it all out. She cried for a while," he remembered, feeling a pang in his heart.

"What did you do?" Carolyn asked, still treating him like a suspect.

"What was I supposed to do? Stand there and watch?" He felt even more defensive of his actions. "I sat by her. I was there for her."

"What does 'there for her' mean?"

"Aw, Mom," he said as he flung his head back, "just never mind, okay? I didn't jeopardize whatever plan you think you have in your head." He turned and began to walk down the hallway to his bedroom.

"It's not my plan, Finn!" she called after him. "And I

don't think it!" she added in a huff.

He rolled his eyes and shut the door. Slumping down on his bed, he pulled out his cell phone to check his messages. Four missed calls. Only three were from Tanya. He sighed. One message was from a prospective client with a new project for him, one was a hang up from Tanya, and on the other two, she actually talked. The first one was snooty. She was at the party; he could hear it in the background.

"Hi Finn, just wanted you to know what you're missing! Stop it, Jesse!" she giggled and the message ended. He rolled his eyes and deleted it and waited for the next one.

"Hi Finn, it's me again. You can ignore my last message. This party blows. I hope you're having fun at the lake. Call me when you get home, all right?" That could be translated to: Jesse is still a jerk and I want you back. He flipped the phone shut, thought for a minute, and then opened it again and dialed Tanya back.

"Finn! Hi!" she exclaimed.

"Hey, Tanya."

"I'm so glad you called! I . . ."

Finn interrupted her. He had a mission. "Yeah, listen, Tanya. I need to say something, all right?"

"Are you okay, baby?" Her excitement dulled.

"Tanya, I just need to be totally honest with you." He drew in a breath and waited for a few seconds and then continued. "I think that you and I should . . . well, I think we should move on."

"What do you mean, move on?"

"I mean that, I don't think we're going to get back together this time." His tone was gentle.

"Oh my God. You're doing this over the phone?" Her anger was loud and clear.

"I'm sorry, I've just," he sighed, frustrated with himself, "I just don't want to drag this out any longer. It's not fair to either of us. There's a reason why we keep breaking up, and I'm tired of fighting it. It's not gonna work. We don't work."

"But Finn!" she cried, "I'm sorry, I know I am demanding, and I expect way too much of you. But you have always been so good to me . . . please, can we just give it one last shot?" Her voice cracked.

"We already did Tanya. I'd just be toying with you, and I don't want to do that."

"Toy with me! I don't care!" she begged. "I just want to be with you!"

"Don't do that Tanya, you are worth more than that. You are."

"Sure. Right," she sniffed dejectedly and then shot back, "You know you'll be back. You always come back."

"Tanya, I'm going to let you go. I'm not going to call you again," he said unapologetically.

"Mmhmm. Sure, Finn. Whatever you say."

Finn rolled his eyes at her know-it-all tone of voice. "All right, well . . . bye Tanya."

"Finn? Wait . . ."

"Yeah?"

"Is there someone else? I mean . . . is there?"

In the amount of time it took for him to blink his eyes, the entire day replayed in his mind. Carrying Allaya back to the cabin, being so incredibly close to her neck—to her—holding her, kissing her while she slept, even pulling down the DVD for her, and, as if Meg Ryan were feeding him lines from that very DVD, he said, "There is the dream of someone else." *Oh my God. I did not just say that. I am such a girl.*

"Nice, Finn. Real nice."

She hung up.

Finn groaned, smacking himself in the forehead. Tanya knew the lines to You've Got Mail backward and forward, since it was her all-time favorite movie. It was an unintentional blow. He had tried his best to let her down easily, but he always seemed to fail where she was concerned.

He flipped the phone shut and sat with his hands on his knees, unwilling to worry about her anymore. He hadn't strung her along. They had broken up weeks ago, and he was just reiterating the point.

It's done.

He laid down on his bed and his mind filled with visions of Allaya. He'd told his mother the truth; he hadn't really done anything stupid. Maybe borderline, but he was still holding back. There were so many ways he'd wanted to express himself to Allaya. He figured that he had made the best choices possible, given the circumstances. Kissing her neck while she slept, well, that may have been a little stupid, but she hadn't been aware of that. He had only made himself suffer in that moment. Telling her he wasn't going anywhere? Well, he couldn't exactly have left without saying something could he? If she had had no idea of his feelings toward her before today, now she would at least have some suspicions. And if she'd had the slightest clue before, then she would know for sure now because of his pledge. He had needed to at least put the thought in her head, and she could choose how to respond to it. He had a feeling, the smallest little hope, that she had picked up on his motives. And if that were the case, she had not shut him down. If anything, he felt encouraged. Maybe he wouldn't have to wait as long as his mother wanted him to.

You're forgetting something.

He shut his eyes, trying to pull his own thoughts in front of the ones that were burning from some unknown place within himself. He remembered the feel of her skin under his fingertips as he traced the curves of her face.

Finn.

Holding her while she sobbed.

That's it. That's what you're forgetting.

Finn opened his eyes, staring at the ceiling.

I brought her here for a reason.

I know that, he responded silently.

I have a plan.

He felt the words more than he heard them, yet they seemed to echo off the walls of his room.

Why do I have to play along? Why should I worry about your plans now?

Because I have a plan for you, too, Finn.

So what? It's never concerned me before.

It has. You just don't remember. And because, Finn, this thing that you want so badly—that you begged for today—as long as you turn from me will never be yours.

"So what? I have to follow you to get the girl?" he growled into the air.

Not exactly how it works. I have good things for you, Finn. A kind of good that you've never seen before. A kind of good that is amazing and beyond your understanding.

"Are we making some kind of deal here? I thought people weren't supposed to try to make deals with God," Finn again said to the empty room.

No deal. Just fact. I love you more than she can. I love her more than you can. She knows that. Do you?

Finn groaned and pulled a pillow over his head.

Do you?

He wasn't prepared to have this encounter.

I'm going to sleep now. He didn't care that it was barely nine o'clock. He was tired, having woken up early and having expended every last ounce of energy trying to keep his hands off of Allaya.

I'm not going anywhere, either.

Eight

Allaya woke with a start. It was still dark outside; she knew it must have still been the middle of the night. She pushed strands of sweat-dampened hair out of her face.

The dream had been so vivid. Marielle was there—smiling, laughing, living—and then out of nowhere she had begun to scream, and, as if being pulled away, her face got smaller and smaller and then had completely disappeared. Allaya saw herself standing in the darkness, her own hair limp and dirty; she looked sick. She was wearing rags—filthy, torn rags—and there were visible scabs and wounds covering her body. After a few moments, a dim light began to shine in the corner of the scene, growing gradually like the sun rising in the eastern sky. As the beams of light reached to her feet, the image of herself began to transform. Her skin went from ashen grey to a pearly cream color. The sores that had covered her legs disappeared. As the light traveled up her body, her rags turned into a beautiful flowing white gown, yards of sheer fabric floated behind her as a breeze began to whip her hair around her face. There was no landscape in the scene, just the light and her transformed being. And then she saw arms wrap around herself from behind. They held her and she felt a physical yearning come from the depths of her being as the arms continued to embrace her, connecting the dream image of herself with her physical being, asleep in the bed. Her likeness in the dream began to cry, softly at first and then in gut-wrenching sobs, as the being behind her swept her up and cradled her.

It's me, Allaya. I'm here. I've got you. I've got you.

His voice soothed her in the very core of her being. She took a breath. Hope and security filled her lungs.

"I need you desperately!" she spoke the words out loud in her sleep.

I know. I love that. One of my favorite things about who you are is that you crave my presence. But you have ignored it for so long, and now, you are awakening to your need again.

"I'm sorry. I don't know how to let go! It hurts so bad. It's going to be so different. I don't know what normal looks like anymore."

I know you feel like a world without Marielle is no world at all, but, Sweet Daughter, a world without both of you would be even worse. She knew what she was getting into. She wasn't scared of death. She was only scared of being lost in a sea of meaningless faces. She wanted to make a difference, to be known by someone. But in holding so tightly to her memory and closing up inside of yourself, Allaya, she has become lost to you, and you lost me, though I have never hidden myself from you. I have something so

beautiful for you, Allaya. Will you come with me?

In her dream Allaya looked up at the blank face of her Savior and as though nothing else mattered in the entire world—because it didn't—she whispered forcefully, "Yes!"

Visions of Herron Lake began to flash through her dream. Finn was there, smiling warmly at her. Her parents and Shara were there, holding their hands out to her. They all seemed to beckon her to draw nearer to them. When she began to feel fear, something squeezed her hand. The Savior was no longer a visible image in the dream, but she knew he was there. She began to walk, as though in front of a green screen, and the scene changed around her. Suddenly she saw herself standing in front of the picture window, staring out at the storm, her towel in a pile on the ground at her feet.

"Ally."

Her eyes opened instantly as she heard her name whispered in her mind, her heart pounding from the exhilaration of the dream. It hadn't been the voice of God that time. To her family she had always been Laya, unless, of course, she'd been in trouble, and then it was always her full name, Allaya Grace Sheldon. But just as she was the only one who called him Finnigan, he was the only one who had ever called her Ally.

"God, what are you doing to me?" she cried out.

Do you trust me?

"I don't know!" She covered her face with her hands, as if trying to hide from him.

Do you believe that I have good gifts for you?

Like what? Like recovery? Reinvention? Her mind screamed while her lips stayed silent.

And more.

I don't deserve more. I just want to be whole again.

Allaya, there is so much that leads to and comes with being whole. Do you believe that—even if you are undeserving—that I will give you good gifts?

I don't know!

Will you let me show you?

I don't know. "Maybe," she said aloud.

I'll wait for you. I'm not going anywhere.

That seemed to be a popular phrase. Finn had said it to her the day before.

Allaya hobbled to the bathroom, holding onto furniture or walls to get there, wincing with each step. She washed her face and got a drink of water. Her brain was flooded with the visions from her dream, trying to make sense of it all. She lay back down on the couch and tried to sleep, but she couldn't turn her brain off, so she finally flipped on the TV and hit play on the DVD remote. She started to feel sleepy again.

"Good night, Dear Void," she whispered and closed her eyes, letting Meg and Tom's email relationship romance her back to sleep.

The TV was still on and the screen blue when Finn let himself in the next morning. Even though it was nine in the morning, Allaya lay sleeping soundly on the couch. Making an effort not to bang any pots and pans this time, Finn found a bag of coffee and brewed a fresh pot. He didn't know if he should wake her, but he didn't want her to be startled like yesterday. He poured two mugs of coffee, grabbed the paper bag he'd brought in, and walked quietly into the living room. He sat on the edge of the coffee table and quietly whispered her name.

"Ally."

She stirred slightly.

"Ally," he said a bit louder. He reached out to touch her arm, started to change his mind, but then touched her anyway. Her arm was cold and soft; her creamy white skin had a hint of a tan coming to surface from her nap in the sun just two days before. He squeezed her arm.

"Ally," he said a third time.

She started to turn over, a soft moan escaping her lips.

"Hmmm?" she stretched her arms over her head.

"Hey, it's me . . . I'm here," he said softly, not wanting a repeat of the previous day.

She squeezed her eyes tight and the corners of her mouth turned up into an embarrassed smile.

"Hi," she said, opening one eye and keeping the other scrunched tight.

"What's up?" he chuckled.

"Um . . . nothing," she sat up and opened her eyes, rubbing them gently. They stung from the tears she'd cried in her sleep through her dream. "What time is it?"

"Nine fifteen."

"Wow! I slept late. How long have you been here?"

"I just got here, I swear. I just made some coffee and woke you up. And I have donuts," he said warily, eyeing the bag on the coffee table.

"Oooh! I want donuts!" She scooted back against the arm of the couch. Finn passed her the bag and took his mug to the recliner.

Allaya pulled out a chocolate glazed donut, and in between bites asked, "You bring the crutches?"

"Yes, I did. Clothes too. They're in the truck."

"Thank you." She took another bite, her eyes rolling back in pleasure. "I love donuts," she sighed, pausing to swallow. Then she asked, "So what are your plans for today?"

"Well," he said slowly, "I found a big log on the side of the road yesterday and I was thinking about stripping the bark off of it today and getting it prepped to take back to the shop in Seattle."

"Oh." She tried not to sound disappointed. She had hoped that he would want to spend more time with her even though she had no concrete plans for herself. *This isn't why I'm here anyway. I need to focus*, she thought.

Ally.

Her head snapped up suddenly and she stared Finn in the face. He choked on a sip of coffee.

"What?" he asked.

"Did you say something?"

He looked at her puzzled and replied, "No . . . ?"

"Never mind," she shook her head and put her lips to the warm mug.

"My tools are in my truck, and I was going to set up by the shore. Do you want to come down with me?"

"Oh! Um," she was surprised by the pounding in her chest, "Yeah, sure."

"It will take me some time to get set up, so, if you need some time to yourself . . ."

She definitely needed a few minutes to gather her thoughts and calm her racing heartbeat. She nodded at him.

"Good," he smiled. "You done?" He glanced at her coffee mug.

"No way. I need at least two cups in order to function today," she responded as a yawn forced itself through her lips.

"Rough night?"

She raised her eyebrows and looked away. "I just had a weird dream. I woke up a lot."

He gave her a curious look but didn't ask any questions. He simply took her mug back to the kitchen and refilled it.

Ten minutes later and safely locked in the bathroom while Finn got his things set up outside by the lake, Allaya turned on the hot water in the tub and let it run over her hand until it reached the temperature she wanted. She sat on the edge and swung her legs around and slowly slid herself in. She winced a little at the hot water but let out a long sigh and laid her head against the shower wall as she relaxed against the back of the tub. She replayed the dream in her mind. There was so much about it that was obvious: she had allowed herself to be identified by her grief over the past two years and it was not attractive. As she released herself to the Lord, he would uncover her inner beauty again. He would reunite her family, and they would be able to move on, together. There would be difficulty still, and pain, but he would be there, and she would finally let him have full access to her life again.

The part that still irked her was that Finn had been part of the dream. She wanted to ignore his role, small as it was, though he was the only other person in the dream who spoke—while she had stood in the window of the cabin, totally naked!

"Uuuugh!" she moaned and slid down so that she was submerged in the steaming hot water.

I have good gifts for you. His voice was like a whisper this time, and her skin prickled in spite of the hot water.

I know! I know! I just . . . I don't know what I'm supposed to do with them!

You will.

Why do you always have to be so cryptic? Why can't you just tell me what is going on? Is it Finn? Is he somehow the missing link? Is he just a mile marker on my journey? You know what? Forget it. I don't want to know. This is too much.

There was no other sound than the water splashing around her as she sat up and blew the air out of her mouth, feeling irritated and stressed.

"Annoyed with God . . . that's going to get me places," she sighed, reaching for the shampoo. The old proverb she'd heard so many times in Sunday school came tumbling into her thoughts:

"Trust in the Lord with all your heart, and lean not on your own understanding; in all your ways submit him, and he will make your paths straight. Proverbs 3:5"

Well, not trusting you hasn't gotten me anywhere either, she reasoned. She scrubbed her face so hard it hurt.

"Fine," she resigned. "Show me. Whatever it is that you wanted to show me, I'm ready." She didn't have the energy to argue with him anymore anyway. There was no thunderstorm or lightning this time, just a sense of peace that she was where she was supposed to be.

Finn knocked on the bathroom door to let her know he had finished setting his tools up. By this time, she had already heaved herself out of the bathtub and was trying to wriggle her damp body into her bikini. She secured a towel around her waist and opened the door.

Finn's eyes grew at the sight of her.

"I know, I just took a bath. I'm not going to get in; I just want to lay out and relax," she said, assuming that his expression had to do with the fact that she'd clearly just been in the tub and was now headed to the lake.

"Okay, whatever you want," he said, swallowing the lump in his throat. He offered her the crutches and dragged his gaze away from her exposed skin, which had been the real reason behind his wide-eyed reaction.

Nothing I haven't seen before, but it almost seems like I'm seeing her for the first time, he thought as he tried to shake the image from his head, turning away from her quickly.

"Actually, that's a good idea! There is a tube down in the shed at the lake. Do you have a rope or something we could tie it to the dock with? Then I could just float on it?"

"Probably. If not, I'm sure there is one around here somewhere."

"Great!" she smiled.

"You seem happy!" he eyed her suspiciously.

"I am. I'm okay," she said with a grin.

"All right!" he said, pleased. "Let's go!"

Finn did his best to walk beside her and spot her, watching out for any holes or branches. It was a short walk down to the dock, but one filled with all kinds of treachery for someone on crutches. He steadied her a few times as they walked down to where Finn's log was set up on two sawhorses on the edge of the bank. He helped Allaya down to the edge of the dock and then loped back up to the truck in search of a rope. She eased herself down to sit, arranging her towel underneath her and stretching her legs out. Finn's footsteps knocked against the wood as he returned and she shielded her eyes to look up at him. The tube he held over his head cast a large shadow over the dock, and Allaya thought she caught a glimpse of something strange in his eyes.

The vision of her laid out like that made him weak in the knees. He was careful not to make eye contact with her and careful not to gawk at the exposed flesh that bulged out of the triangles of her swimsuit.

"The tube is pretty dirty. There are some webs and dead bugs in the bottom." He squinted as he looked down on her.

She had a coy look on her face as she fluttered her eyelashes at him. He cursed her in his head.

"Oh brother," he rolled his eyes and shifted uncomfortably, "I wasn't going to make you clean it out!"

She grinned and watched as he put the tube down, dropped the rope beside it and stripped off his T-shirt. Allaya drew in a sharp breath. Widening her eyes, she quickly turned her gaze toward the lake, hoping he hadn't heard her gasp. He was lean, but the six-pack had not been an illusion. He was strong, his skin flawless with only a small patch of hair in the middle of his chest.

Oh my gosh, he's beautiful! Allaya felt the familiar knots start forming in her stomach, her cheeks reddening. *Is that what you wanted to show me? I'll take that gift! Wow.*

She turned over onto her stomach to watch him as he bent down and dipped his T-shirt in the water, squeezed it out and wiped the tube down. The sun shone on his back; his muscles stretched as he kneeled over the inner tube. Allaya bit her bottom lip and squeezed her eyes shut, embarrassed that after all these years, she was finally seeing Finn for what he really was—no longer a silly boy, but a man. An attractive man.

"All right. All clean!" He turned around and grinned at

her.

"Uh thanks," she stammered nervously, starting to lift herself off the dock.

"Hold on! I'll help you! Just a minute!" He secured one end of the rope to the tube and the other to the dock and then tossed the tube in, letting it drift in the water. He then turned to help her up.

She sat on her knees as Finn took her arms and stood as her balance while she pulled herself up the rest of the way. He wrapped his arm around her waist; his heartbeat quickening as his fingers grazed bare skin around her midsection.

"So, um," he said carefully, "how are we going to do this?" He looked down at her, concentrating on keeping eye contact.

"What?" She looked surprised. "Do what?"

"Uh . . . you want to get in that tube right? The one that I just washed out for you?"

"Oh," she laughed nervously, "that! Um, I'm not sure." She'd become completely distracted by the feeling of his calloused fingers on her skin. She'd forgotten all about the tube.

"Well, let's see. Do you think you can go a few steps down on the ladder? Like, if you sit here," he motioned toward the space between the ladder handles, "and put your foot on the second rung, and then turn around? I'll hold onto the tube and keep it steady."

"Yeah, I think that'll work." Allaya sat down in between the arm rails and Finn pulled the tube back in toward the dock, dragging it toward her. She found the second step with her uninjured foot, and rotated around so her back was to the tube and she was facing Finn.

"So I'll just, uh, reach around . . ." Finn was on his knees and had to reach both arms around her in order to hold on to the tube so she could slip back into it. Their faces were so close that he could feel her breath on his cheek; the touch of her skin on his arm was like fire that burned all the way into his lungs. He had the sides of the tube in his grip, and he peeked around her to make sure it was close enough to her. He wasn't sure there was a way he could be any closer to her at all . . . well, there was one.

"I think we're good," he said, quickly dismissing the thought. But at that moment, he steadied himself and looked up. She was mere inches away from him, staring at him, her lips pressed so tightly together that they were turning white and her eyes wide. He could feel the heat from her body, even where he wasn't touching her. Then there was that fresh shampoo scent again.

He was mere seconds away from completely losing himself, from indulging deeply in the desires of his heart, or his flesh, or both, and she made no attempt to put distance between them or to get into the tube. She was frozen

Nine

Allaya's blood stopped flowing and started running in circles, or at least, that was what it felt like. Her heart raced and she squeezed her lips so tight they hurt. She could feel his breath, and as close as he was to her, she felt as though she was being pulled closer still. She hadn't felt this electricity in years.

It hadn't been this intense with Matthew. For the split second while she and Finn stared each other down, she wondered why it hadn't. There had been butterflies with Matthew, but never a longing.

What if this is just physical? What if it fades? Am I really okay with this? Oh crap, what am I doing? she thought. There wasn't any more time for her inner dilemma. His right hand had let go of the tube and was pressing on the small of her back, pressing her even closer to him. She was almost certain there would be burn marks left in her skin from his touch. Her breath caught in her throat as she stared into his eyes. She was overwhelmed by the stirring in her stomach, the warmth that was spreading through her body as she gave in to the pressure from his hand.

Finn's expression seemed as startled as she felt, his eyes wide and searching, "Ally."

She shushed him by closing the last of the distance between them and pressed her lips against his. The electric current that ravaged her body as he responded to her rendered her completely unaware of anything else other than his lips on hers. She let go of the ladder with one arm and wrapped it around his neck as his lips parted hungrily against hers. He lifted her up and out of the water with his strong arms. The jagged wood from the dock dug in to her knees as she straddled him, but she barely felt it.

Finn tore his lips from hers and began kissing her chin, her cheeks, underneath her jawbone.

She was exploding on the inside, feeling safer in his arms than she had felt in years, but at the same time, well aware of the danger that presented itself. A tingling sensation lingered in the places where his lips met her skin, leaving her breathless.

Finn knew he needed to find an ounce of control somewhere in his body. He slowed himself, returned his lips to hers and held them in one spot, unmoving. Reluctantly, he tilted his head down so that his forehead was touching hers, and his nose was pressed on her cheek.

"Ally. Oh my God, Ally." He could feel the rise and fall of her chest against his as she buried her face in his shoulder, her breath tickling the skin on his chest. He breathed in deeply against her neck. He wanted nothing more than to continue to explore her body, to memorize every inch of her skin. Instead, he sighed and gently pushed her away but not so far that he had to remove his hands from her hips. He couldn't jeopardize this. Maybe he already had.

"Finn," she looked at him apologetically, her eyes wet with unshed tears.

"No. Allaya, I'm sorry, I shouldn't have pushed you like that." He hung his head.

"Pushed me? You did not push me. I practically ran you over!" She smiled softly as a tear trickled down the corner of her eye.

He was in agony. *Why is she crying?* He reached up with his forefinger and caught the tear on his fingertip.

"Don't waste this on me," he said, and kissed the teardrop off of his finger.

Her breath caught in her throat.

"Ally, I have to be honest with you," he said grimly.

She felt the icy cold fingers of fear wrap around her heart. Those were never good words. She was still precariously perched with her legs around him, and the heat passing between them had nothing to do with the August sun that shone from the cloudless sky above them.

"What?" she whispered, her voice cracking.

I thought this was part of it, Lord? I mean . . . wasn't that what you meant? Now what? She cringed, biting her lip again, bracing herself for the blow.

"I should have told you before. I didn't mean to . . ."

"Finn, just tell me." She took his face in her hands and pleaded with him.

"The night of the storm," he started.

She furrowed her brows nervously.

The storm? He was with me after that, what could he possibly have to tell me about that night? Wait. After he left? Maybe he met someone . . . but then, why . . . ?

"I was out on the lake . . ."

"You got caught in the rain," she stated.

"Yes, I did, but . . . something else sort of . . . happened. I wasn't completely honest with you that night."

Ally looked up into the sky, not caring to shield her eyes from the sun. She felt a rise of emotion welling up in her eyelids and it was all threatening to spill out.

How could I have misread all the things that you said, Lord? The dream? He was in it. He said my name! I don't understand! She heaved in a huge breath and looked back at Finn.

Seeing the pain in her face was torture for him. Surely she would run—well, hobble—away from him; call him disgusting and vile, perverted. But he had to tell her. He was one up on her, and she needed to know that. He kept trying to remind himself that he was a stand-up kind of guy.

"Go on," she said flatly. Where could he possibly be going with this? She wished that she could pull herself out of his lap, but there was really nowhere to go but into the water that was lapping the dock.

"I was already off of the lake when the rain hit. I had already tied up the boat and was on my way up the dock when the rain started pouring."

Allaya was confused. What could this have to do with anything?

Finn squinted his eyes as he avoided her gaze and stared across the lake. "I didn't mean to, I mean, I wasn't expecting it at all, and once it happened, I couldn't stop . . ." He reached down and picked up a small piece of wood that had splintered off of the dock, breaking it into smaller pieces between his fingers.

The night in question flashed before her eyes: she was standing at the window. Then her perspective changed and she was envisioning her dream again. In her dream, she had seen herself in the window from the outside, not from the actual perspective she'd had in real time during the storm, and instantly she knew.

"You saw me."

"I saw you."

They spoke in unison.

His head snapped back to stare at her, "H-how did you know?"

Her face turned crimson. "Wow. I um . . . Oh, wow. I can't really explain that right now, but . . . oh my gosh." Then she started to laugh, and she covered her face with her hands and leaned into his shoulder again.

It was Finn's turn to be confused. "You're not upset?" He pulled back and gave her a puzzled look.

"No, not really. I mean . . . it was my own fault for being so dimwitted. Of course, I didn't expect that anyone would be outside in that kind of storm so, I guess maybe a little bit . . . but . . . no, not really." She tilted her head, speaking as she processed her thoughts, her cheeks still pink but her eyes dancing with amusement.

"You're not upset that I stood out here on this dock for like . . . thirty minutes ogling at your naked body in the pouring rain? While you had no clue?"

"Well, when you put it like that I am!" She smacked his arm and pulled herself back onto the ladder. "Thirty minutes? In the rain? Wow," she giggled.

"Ally, I'm serious! You should be repulsed by me!"

She gripped his hand and pulled it to her chest. "I'm not," she said as another tear slid down her cheek.

"Why are you crying?" She was driving him mad, and her skin was burning underneath his hand.

"Because it makes sense now. Or at least, some of it does . . ."

"What are you talking about? What makes sense?"

"It's hard to explain. I have to process a little more before I can really try," she said, shaking her head.

"You are so confusing, Allaya Sheldon." He pulled his hand from hers, sulking a bit that she hadn't been enraged by his betrayal like he had expected—like he deserved. At least if she had been angry with him and had ordered him away, he'd have to leave her alone.

"Trust me. No one knows that better than I do, Finnigan." She brushed the tear from her eye and looked at him playfully as she sniffled, "So, the whole storm? Really?"

He blushed, but his face was serious. "I couldn't help myself Ally. You were like . . . this . . . angel of light or something, and I just could not stop staring at you. I couldn't get enough. Man that sounds so ridiculous."

She laughed out loud. "I'm not sure angels are actually naked, but uh, I'll take it, I guess."

"Well, it was pitch black, yours was the only light on, and you were just there and . . . oh, never mind," he said again, crossing his arms and looking away.

Allaya inched herself closer to him again, empowered by his response to her; she enjoyed playing the part of the captor. She pried his arms apart and positioned herself between them.

"I'm not mad, Finn."

"Yeah. Well, you should be. We've been friends for years. You're practically my sister, and we just—oh God, we just—" his own cheeks burned with embarrassment.

"Oh, please Finn. We just *kissed*. We didn't do anything wrong, and even if we weren't planning on pursuing this, we haven't crossed any line that we couldn't re-cross."

"You . . . you want to pursue this?" The hope and the doubt were obvious in his voice.

"You are a good man, Finnigan. A good . . . gift." She paused as the truth in her words took root. The smile hit her eyes first and then spread over her face, "And I don't know what this is. It's scary and strange, and . . . good." A wealth of emotions crossed through her expression as she tried to work out what that kiss meant. "I mean, didn't that feel good?" She felt as surprised as he looked.

"You're really not mad?"

She smiled softly and shook her head, "I just can't believe this is happening now, after all these years!"

Finn's eyes widened in agreement. "I know! I *never* thought about you like that, *ever!*"

Allaya's jaw dropped. "Well, gee, thanks!" she said with a smirk.

"What about you?" he asked.

"Me?"

"Yeah, did you think about me like that?" He gave her a quizzical look.

"Oh, please, Finn. Who didn't think about you like that at least once? Of course I had a crush on you, until you went and dashed all my hopes and dreams with Shara!"

"Am I ever going to hear the end of it?" His hands rested on her hips again, just above the waistline of her bikini.

She grinned at him. "I'm pretty sure I'll be able to let it go, as long as . . ." she trailed off.

"As long as what?" He leaned forward in earnest.

"As long as you didn't kiss her like that!" she said, pointing to her lips.

His face paled. "I swear to God, Allaya, I didn't."

She laughed silently and laid her hand on his cheek. "Like you said, that was years ago. It doesn't matter now. But this does. I feel it."

Finn pressed his cheek hard into her hand, turning his face to kiss her wrist. "I don't deserve you, Ally."

"After the last two years, I definitely don't deserve you," she sighed.

He looked up at her, his eyes soft and searching. "Where do we go from here? I mean you're dealing with all this emotional stuff, and I don't want to pressure you into something."

"I don't know for sure, but I'm actually not worried about it," she said, surprised that it was the truth.

"I've lived a lot of life since we were kids, and I've made choices that might change things for you"

She shook her head. "They won't, Finn."

"No, I mean . . ."

"I know what you mean," she interrupted. "I'm not proud of it, but I'm not a virgin either. I was on the verge of being engaged, Finn. It happened." She'd never told anyone that before. Just another item on her list of things to deal with during her week of solitude, which was quickly taking a completely different direction than she'd ever hoped or imagined.

"Ass," he muttered under his breath, remembering how that Matthew guy had abandoned Allaya. "So is that something that's . . . um . . . on the table?" He stammered, hoping.

"No. I'm not that girl anymore," she sighed. "I don't know who I am, but I'm not that girl."

"Oh, okay," he smiled sheepishly. "Can't blame me for asking, can you?"

She smiled and leaned in to kiss him again. He moaned softly but did not fight her. Their lips met only briefly this time, but it was enough to send shivers down his spine.

"Damn, Ally," Finn whispered as he pulled away and pushed her hair behind her ears, "how did this happen?" He shook his head, gazing into her eyes.

"I can only guess," she whispered.

"It's unreal. It's surreal, it's—"

"It's unbelievable," she sighed.

He trailed his fingers up her arm.

"If I kiss you again," he said as though in warning.

"Don't," she said quietly and pulled away.

He nodded. "Yeah. You're right. I need to put some distance between myself and," he gestured toward her, "all that!"

Allaya had some pity on him and scooted aside. He stood to gather the rope and pull the tube back in.

"I think I'm gonna forego the tube today."

"Are you sure? I cleaned it for you."

"Wasn't it worth it?" she blushed.

He grinned from ear to ear.

"I suppose so. Wait! Was this all part of some diabolical plan? Make me work hard for my payoff?" He reached for her hands to help her up.

She laughed out loud at him; her cheeks were starting to hurt from smiling so much.

"Hardly! I just clued in to this whole thing not too long ago."

"You and me both," he whispered and he did kiss her one last time.

She lost herself in the feeling of his arms wrapped tightly around her waist, their bodies pressed against each other. She could have stayed lost all day, but he released her quickly, parted his lips from hers and said, "All right. I'm going to go up there," and gestured with his eyes toward the sawhorses, "and you need to stay down here. Deal?"

"Deal."

"And you are never allowed to be that naked in front of me again unless—"

"I got it, Finn." She felt her cheeks burn. Finn walked her back to where she had been sitting before and eased her down onto the towel.

As he walked away he called back, "This would have been so much easier if you hadn't have sprained your damn ankle!"

Allaya smiled and laid her head against the old planks of the dock.

None of this is easy, she thought to herself, *except for the part where I'm suddenly myself again. Imagine that. Who knew Finn was such a good kisser? Oh, right. Shara.* She rolled her eyes and laughed quiet.

Ten

Finn felt that he deserved a pat on the back, an award, some kind of acknowledgement for the feat he had just accomplished. It had taken every fiber in his being to pull himself away from her, to have had his hands on her like he had fantasized and then to have removed them without actually fulfilling the entire fantasy.

In spite of that, to the core of his being he felt relieved that he was not alone in his fight—that she was reciprocating whatever it was that was going on between them. As he slaved over the huge tree, scraping and discarding large chunks of bark, he anticipated the next opportunity he might have to put his hands on her again, when he could breathe in her scent. He had to steady himself against the sawhorses and catch his breath.

I need water. Cold water.

He put his tool down and grabbed his water bottle from the ground, and turned his gaze to the dock where Allaya was baking in the sun. She was lying sideways against the width of the dock, the outline of her body a sharp contrast to dark color of the lake and mountainous backdrop. She must have sensed him watching her. She fidgeted a little, and then slowly lifted her head in his direction with her hand shielding her eyes. He turned away quickly, embarrassed that he'd been caught. He rolled his eyes at himself and took a swig of water.

Allaya laughed to herself as she lay her head back down and let out a sigh. She was still reeling from their passionate embrace, feeling a little giddy about the whole thing. It was so strange to feel anything other than depression, and she reveled in the joy of feeling like herself again—or a new version of herself. The fact that it had been Finn who had unlocked that vault had caught her completely off guard. For the past two years, Allaya had convinced herself that the only thing she could succeed at was holding on to her pain, holding on to Marielle's memory like an alcoholic with a bottle of liquor. She thought that holding on would be the only way to survive.

But she realized now that she hadn't been surviving at all. She had been dying from the inside out, drowning in sorrow and grief. But now it was as if she had just come up for air for the first time since Marielle died. As the sun beat down, she imagined herself being transformed, just like in her dream. She imagined herself becoming beautiful again, the wounds fading.

You never stopped being beautiful, my love. You were just hidden under a whole bunch of ugliness. It was never you.

I think I get that now. I think I understand now, she thought.

I have so much more to show you. We are only at the beginning of this journey.

Is Finn along for the ride? Is he really a part of this trip?

He is a part of this trip, but whether or not he is along for the ride is completely up to him.

Allaya was puzzled. For the first time in a long time, she was experiencing conversation with God as clearly as if he sat beside her in the flesh, and she wondered what the last answer meant.

He and I have some unfinished business.

What does that mean? You won't let him come along if he doesn't . . . what? Comply with your commands?

You know better than that, Allaya. None of my children are without the need for my grace, my forgiveness, and my love. He won't be enough for you without me. He can't even begin to love you like I do.

Love?

Yes, dear. Love.

She felt a knot form in her belly, a troubling in her spirit. She sat up and looked towards the bank where Finn was working over the log. He was in the shadows of the trees, but she could still see the sweat glistening on his back, the muscles in his arms working overtime as he reshaped the log.

He's not . . .with you?

Not yet.

Her heart plummeted. *Well, what now? What am I supposed to do?*

It's not up to you, my love; it's up to him. You can't persuade him in either direction. His motives would be off. He and I have some unfinished business.

Yeah, you said that. She took a deep breath and rested her head on the knee of her uninjured leg. *But what about*—she relived their kiss, or kisses, rather. Her heart quickened while she remembered his touch on her back, his lips on her neck.

You're a big girl, Allaya. A strong woman. You will know what to do and when you need to do it.

I don't think I am that strong, Father.

I am.

She willed herself not to cry again. She didn't want to cry anymore. She felt confused, and a little angry.

All of this would have been helpful to know beforehand, she thought.

Allaya groaned when there was no response and laid back down with her hands over her eyes. She was at a loss. She felt the familiar darkness beginning to seep back into her mind.

Allaya. The call was so clear, as if he was speaking to her through the sky. **Allaya.**

"What?" she hissed.

Do not lose hope. I have good gifts for you.

"Yeah, yeah."

She turned her face away from the sun, toward the cabin and toward Finn. He looked as though he was packing things up. It was probably almost noon, she estimated by the position of the sun. She sat up again and continued to watch him wistfully, and began to remember how things had felt with Matthew. There was a similar kind of build-up, anticipation, and chemistry. But there was something so different about what was happening to her now. She felt drawn to Finn in a way that seemed bigger than her. It had to be supernatural; it was the only explanation. It had never been like that with Matthew. She hadn't ever doubted, even years later, that she had loved him, but she had recognized that their love had been seriously lacking.

Suddenly though, she began to wonder if it had really

been love at all. Not that she was necessarily in love with Finn—not even close—but definitely, absolutely, physically charged, attracted and connected to him. Even when she and Matthew had slept together, there hadn't been a chemistry so strong as what she had just experienced with Finn. She imagined what making love to Finn would be like, and quickly regretted the thought for the desire that it stirred inside of her body.

She and Matthew had slept together the night after they had officially talked about marriage, the night after her last journal entry. It hadn't been something she'd planned on happening, but they had been pushing the limits for months. One of them had always had to gather the strength to stop things before they got too far, but on that night, they'd both given in. Matthew had skimmed his fingers across her midriff, giving her the signal that he wanted to make out and she'd responded immediately. When it came time for one of them to put the brakes on, neither of them did. He told her how much he loved her, and how he couldn't wait until he could marry her. Her heart had swelled beneath his body and she clung on to the image of the two of them growing old together as they spiraled down into a chasm that neither one of them wanted to climb out of.

While it had been very typical of what she knew the first time would be, it had also been a very passionate experience, and she hated that she looked back on it with shame. She had truly believed that she would marry him, but that didn't make it right. She knew that when it happened and she knew it now, but somehow it had been enough for her back then. It was only a few days later that they learned about Marielle, and it was a month after that when Matthew left.

"Uuuugh," she sighed. "I do not need to go there again."

She shook her head and began to gather up her things.

Finn was making his way down to her. She immediately felt a knot pull in her stomach as he approached, more from caution than desire—not that desire wasn't there also.

"I'm packed up. You wanna go get some lunch?"

"Yes, definitely. But I have to do one thing first." She held out her hand to him.

He clasped it, immediately pleased by her touch. "What's that?" He pulled her to her feet carefully.

"I have to get a stone."

"A stone?" He looked puzzled, but then he remembered and tilted his head to the side curiously. "You are still doing that? I mean, didn't you guys finish the garden years ago?"

"Yeah, we did, but this is for something different." She looked at her hands.

"What is it for?"

"Um, well . . . a memorial," she said quietly.

"Ally," he sighed.

"I have to do this. This is the last time that I'm going to say goodbye to her. I have to." She was maintaining her composure, but not well.

Finn put his arms around her and held her tightly. "That will mean so much to your family, and it would have meant so much to her," he said into her hair. He felt his shirt dampen with her tears, and he tilted her head toward his. He kissed each of her cheeks directly on the path that her tears were taking.

She leaned back into him without saying a word, feeling overwhelmed by all the emotions stirring inside of her.

"Do you want me to do it for you, or are you going in?" he asked.

She dried her eyes and said, "I need to do it, but I think I need you to help."

"I will do whatever you need me to."

They walked back to the ladder. This time he went first and helped guide her as she struggled into the water. She found her footing but kept a tight grip on his arm.

"This stupid ankle," she cursed.

"Is it any better?"

"A little, I suppose, but I still can't put any weight on it. If I could, I could just pick up a stone with my toes.

Finn laughed. "I forgot about your incredibly talented feet,"

"Did you also forget that I can peel a banana faster with my toes than you can with your hands?" Allaya grinned.

"I told you then, and I'll tell you again, Allaya Sheldon, that's not something to brag about."

Allaya giggled and steadied herself on his arm.

"Are you gonna go under?" he asked.

"Yeah, it's not that deep. Just stay close, this will probably hurt."

"I'll be right here. Not going anywhere . . . remember?" his eyes twinkled and she smiled softly at him, her stomach fluttering.

"I remember." She took a deep breath and dove down into the water, opening her eyes in spite of the sting it caused. She clenched her fists as pain shot through her ankle as she kicked at the water, but she pressed on in search of two stones—one to make up for the previous day and one for the current one.

Finn watched her swim around from above water; she continued to embody something angelic. Her hair flowed behind her; she could have been a mermaid this time. She disappeared from sight for a few seconds as she pushed to the bottom of the lake for a larger stone and then surfaced, gasping for air. Her dark hair, now even darker from being wet, was slicked back from the weight of the water and hung as one solid piece down her back. She reached for his arm and he pulled her in toward the dock.

"God, you are so beautiful," he said.

She was a bit hesitant as he pulled her toward him, but she allowed herself to be drawn in. She had nowhere else to go, for he was her support. He planted his feet on the rocky bottom and leaned against one of the wooden posts supporting the dock, and pulled her to him in much the same way he had held her earlier.

"Lunch, remember?" she said nervously, clasping her hands behind his head.

"Yes. Lunch. In a minute." He pushed a runaway bunch of wet hair from her temple and let his hands slide down her back. She shuddered.

"Goose bumps," he chuckled.

"Yeah, yeah. I wear my feelings on my skin, I guess," she sighed and rolled her eyes.

He kissed her shoulder. "I'm glad. If you didn't, I would have never known."

Allaya tried to remain on the defensive, but with her arms wrapped around him and his hands smoothing themselves against her skin, he was quickly wearing down her will to fight. She wanted to wrap her legs around him and sink into one of his kisses.

"Gosh, Finnigan," she sighed. "When did you get so irresistible?"

"Same time as you, I suppose. Standing in the rain, oblivious to the fact that I was being soaked to the bone, staring up at the most beautiful thing I had ever seen in my entire life." He tightened his arms around her and again drew her into him, kissing her so tenderly, so softly, she nearly stopped breathing. She tightened her grasp on him too. There was no space, no air, no water between them. The electric currents were buzzing through her veins again. A force stronger than gravity seemed to pull them together.

This is so amazing, so, unbelievable, so . . . fun! she thought to herself as her lips parted on his. *Do we really need to eat? I could stay here . . . forever.* She engaged deeper, her fingers tangled in his hair, and she finally let her legs wrap tightly around him. She could *feel* him . . .

Allaya.

She tensed up and froze. The moment was gone, and she was only slightly thankful. Part of her wished they could indulge themselves just a little longer, but she'd heard the Father loud and clear. She carefully unwrapped herself from his grip and pulled away from him, reaching for the ladder rungs for support.

Finn remained in the water for a moment, his head leaning against the post.

"Lunch?" he whispered with his eyes still closed.

"Lunch," she said and heaved herself up onto the dock.

Allaya was careful to keep herself in check when they got back to the cabin. She pulled on a T-shirt and shorts and they made sandwiches side by side quietly. She directed him to the fridge for sodas and then they sat at the table across from one another. Finn started to chuckle after a few bites.

He wiped his mouth with his hand and choked out, "Do you remember when we hog-tied Benjamin Morgan to that old fallen tree in the woods?"

"Oh my gosh. Yes!" Allaya burst into giggles. "We were so mean!"

"Aw, hell! The kid got what he deserved! He was a bratty little turd! I bet he's in jail now!"

"Why did we do that again? I can't remember!"

"You don't remember the mud ball he threw at the back of Marielle's head? The frog he wrapped in your towel?"

"Oh yeah! I guess he did deserve it," She laughed. "Man, he yelled and cried for hours! I can't believe we just left him there all alone!

"I got in so much trouble, but at the end of the day, I went to bed with a huge grin on my face! And he never bothered us again, did he?"

"What about when your cousin was here that summer? What was his name?"

"Kent."

"Right, Kent. Every day he'd go streaking up and down the docks!" Allaya started to laugh so hard she snorted her drink up her nose.

"Oh, I'll *never* forget that," he grinned. "Those old ladies on the beach shrieking and yelping! He has a wife and a little girl now, but he's still the funniest guy I've ever known!" Finn leaned back on his chair and smiled at the memories. "Once he even talked me into streaking with him you know," he nodded with a sly grin.

"Really?" Allaya's eyes danced. "Guess I missed out, huh?"

"Yeah, you guys had already left by then. Good thing, too. It probably would have ruined my chances with you."

"You didn't even know you had a chance with me." She crossed her arms and eyed him mischievously.

"I do now, though, don't I?" He winked.

Her breath caught in her throat and she looked down at her plate.

"Man! We've got a boatload of memories, don't we?" He reached forward and locked fingers with hers.

"Speaking of boats . . ." She looked at him sideways with a wide grin. Finn pulled away from her hand and sat back with his hands raised in defense.

"Aw, come on. Don't go there."

"You know you should never drink and drive!" her eyes shone as she teased him.

Finn groaned and grabbed his plate, heading for the sink. "Fine! You win! Let's not relive it!" he pleaded.

"Imagine our surprise," she started in a singsong voice as he dropped his head into his hands, "just laying out on the dock, my sisters and I, minding our own business, when all the sudden we hear a loud crack come from the south end of the lake. Everyone on the dock jumps up to see what's happened, and some idiot and his friends have totally flipped a familiar-looking speedboat upside down in the water and have barely escaped with their lives, mind you! Oh, wait! That was *you* wasn't it?" Allaya laughed.

He shook his head. "Not my finest moment."

"Well, it was scary back then . . . for a few minutes. Then it was hysterical, and it's still pretty funny!" she giggled.

"Definitely a day to remember, but what you don't

remember is that that was the week we got the prognosis on my dad," he said, sobering.

Allaya's smile faded. "Really? Oh, Finnigan, I'm sorry!"

"Oh, no, it's no big deal. It's been years ya know? But, I was acting out then. I was, I dunno, expressing myself or something," he said dismissively and then stood and rinsed off his plate.

"Does it still hurt?" Allaya was looking down at her hands.

"Does what still hurt?"

"Not having your dad around."

"Oh. That," he paused and carefully considered his words. "Well, we had a pretty superficial relationship. Don't get me wrong, we got along and did guy stuff sometimes, but we just weren't super close. I guess it doesn't really hurt anymore. I mean, I wish he was still here and all that, but I'm fine."

Allaya was silent.

"It was nothing like you and Marielle, Ally. You can't compare the two situations. And it's been years for me."

"I know. I was just wondering," she said quietly.

Finn reached over and squeezed her hand. "My mom said that there will always be pain where Marielle should be but that eventually it will ease itself a bit. Or something like that."

"I love your mom. She's so great."

Finn snorted, "Yeah, she's a charmer that one!" He pulled his hand away. His mother seemed to have a knack for reserving her best qualities for everyone but him. He supposed that that was the job of a mother though, to drive her children crazy. "So what's your plan for the rest of the day?" he asked, changing the subject.

"I don't know. I didn't really have any plans being here, and now with my ankle, I'm kind of limited anyway."

"Well, do you want to go see a movie or something? That's the only thing I can think of that won't require too much mobility on your part."

"We could do that. It might be good to disassociate for a bit . . . from my thoughts, I mean, not from you!" she added quickly.

"Well, I'll call and see what kind of matinees they've got in town."

An hour later Ally was settled in the passenger side of Finn's truck and they were on their way to town.

"This is fun," she said.

"What is?"

"Being with you. Being here. Remembering old times."

Finn reached for her and held her hand. "I didn't plan on this you know," he said quietly.

"I know."

"No really. I mean, my mom called me last week and asked me to come. She said you would be here, and, for some reason, I knew that nothing was going to stop me from being here." He paused to glance at her and her expression didn't change. "I didn't know what it was, but I had to be here. I definitely did not expect any of this to happen though." He motioned between them.

"So, what—you were compelled to be here?"

"I guess you could say that."

She didn't respond but lapsed into a thoughtful silence.

They sat close during the movie, an Adam Sandler comedy that kept them in hysterics for most of its duration.

Finn held her hand securely in his own. He was glad for the comedic outbursts, even if they were the only ones in the theater laughing. If they'd seen a dramatic film he would have lost interest in the plot and would have done his best to distract Allaya, as well.

She was content to let him hold her hand and lose herself in the story. For the most part, everything felt right about being with him. Her hand fit perfectly inside his. The only red flags she had were the ones that had been raised during her last inner dialogue, and she hadn't felt she'd been given enough direction to put a pause on things with Finn. As long as they kept themselves and their bodies in check, everything would be fine. At least that's what she told herself.

Finn drove her back to the cabin and walked her up the steps after the movie ended. "I hate to say this, but I really need to get back to mom's to help her a bit today. That is why I came after all, and, though I would much rather be here with you, believe me, I know it's hard for her to do this all by herself."

"Don't worry about it. I wish I could come help! But truthfully, I do need some time to myself. I've got to . . . well, you know. I've got to get my crap together before I head back to the city this weekend. Or at least make a good effort."

"Yeah, I know."

"What about after dinner tonight? You won't be working then right?"

"No, probably not. Mom's pretty hooked on her shows. You know, all the CSIs and whatever else," he rolled his eyes.

"Well, if you want to come back tonight, we can watch TV or hang out, or whatever."

"Are you sure? I don't want to crowd you or anything."

"Finnigan, I can only handle so much time by myself. I think it's divine intervention that you are here this week!" She said it lightly, but the weight of her words was not lost on either of them.

"Good," he grinned. "I'll come by around seven?"

"Sure. Save room for dessert!" she winked.

"I will." He handed her the crutches he'd carried up for her and reached around to give her a hug. All he needed from her was a signal. Her arms slid over his shoulders, her head buried in his neck. He heard her sigh. That was what he was looking for. He pulled his head back and looked into her eyes hungrily. She made the move. She used her hand to pull his head to hers. Overtaken, he pressed her into the door and took control of her mouth. A small sigh escaped her lips in between movements and he took it as encouragement. She was squeezing his neck too tightly for him to back away from her anyway. He pressed himself into her harder and hoisted her up around his hips again. That was when she protested. He carefully slid her back down and untangled his lips from hers.

"What?" he begged, searching her eyes.

"You've got to stop doing that to me," she sighed with her eyes closed and her head against the door. Her heart was pounding so hard she was surprised that Finn couldn't hear the buzz of her blood coursing through her vein; it was deafening in her own ears.

"Me? You kissed me!" he exclaimed.

"Not that. The wrapping me around yourself thing." She was breathless, and he appeared hurt. "It's too much, Finn. Too much too fast. It's too intense." She smoothed her T-shirt out against her waist, fidgeting with the hem.

"Oh," he said, his pride wounded.

"I feel like I could kiss you forever, Finn. But when you do that, it's just not enough but yet it's too much at the same time. Does that make any sense?" she laughed nervously.

He nodded with understanding, his hurt and embarrassment eased for the moment. "So, I turn you on, huh?" he smiled a devilish grin.

"Um . . . ha . . . uh . . . yes. So, stop it!" She slapped his arm.

"Baby, I can try, but I can't make any promises!" he said smoothly and raised his eyebrows, looking at her sideways.

"Oh my word, Finnigan. Go home!" She rolled her eyes at him.

"All right. Fine, I'll go. But just you remember, I'm coming back for you," he said in a saucy voice.

"I'll wear my sexiest sweatpants!" she retorted. He laughed and turned on his heel, his pride restored.

Eleven

Allaya watched him drive away and then slowly closed the door. She stood for a minute waiting for her stomach to calm down, for her insides to stop raging. Her eyes were huge as she relived each time their lips had met. After all those years . . .

She looked around the kitchen, trying to decide what her next step should be. She could sit and try to sort through her feelings, but she knew by the nervousness in her stomach that what she was feeling could not be sorted just yet. She tried to scold herself for letting things progress so quickly, but as she replayed the moments in her head again to try to prepare herself for his next move, she found herself dwelling, blushing, smiling, and giggling even.

I feel alive again, she thought, and her smile grew even wider.

She didn't know how long she stood in the kitchen staring into space, smiling like a goon, but her cheeks began to hurt so she picked up the novel she'd brought along just in case she needed an escape from the real reason she had come up to the lake. She hoped to distance herself from the warmth that lingered where Finn's hands had touched her and where she could still feel his kisses, but a few pages in she realized that reading a romance novel was not going to help her cause any.

She sighed, got up from the table, and hobbled around the cabin a bit, straightening pillows and folding the blanket she had slept under the night before. She hopped down the hall to put it away and stopped short at the door to the room the three girls had shared every summer and stared at the closed door. She knew that before the week was up, she'd have to go into that room and face the painful memories there. She'd been trying to prepare herself for that step, but she wasn't there yet. She pressed her hand against the door, closed her eyes and drew in a breath.

"Not today," she whispered.

Finn arrived promptly at seven o'clock. Allaya answered the door as promised—in sweats—and there he was, with a small bouquet of wild flowers for her.

"I really am a gentleman!" he said, bowing.

"Nice touch!" she smiled and shut the door behind him. He found a glass to put the flowers in while she pulled brownies out of the oven.

"Not exactly gourmet, but . . . I didn't really plan on company when I went to the store and packed my supplies," she said.

"Compared to Twinkies, brownies are gourmet!" he grinned.

Allaya made a face. "I forgot about you and Twinkies!"

"A match made in heaven!"

"Blech," she cringed.

"I feel the same way about those sweatpants," he said, eyeing them as if they were to be feared.

"Oh, come on! I dressed up for you!" she said playfully.

He simply rolled his eyes and then glanced between she and the brownies.

Allaya slapped his hand away as he reached for them. "They have to cool for a few minutes!" Shooing him into the living room, she set the brownies on the table.

"Speaking of cooling," Finn began as he sat down in the recliner, "I need to apologize to you."

"For what?"

"For today. For taking too much liberty with you, for pushing you, for . . ." he looked down at his hands, his cheeks a little red.

"Oh-ho-ho no! No way. No way do you get to take all the responsibility for that one," she waved a finger at him.

"I know, Ally, I know, but you had to stop me, and, I just, I want you know that I am sorry about that. You won't have to do that again. See? I'm here on this extremely uncomfortable recliner versus the couch with you."

"That stupid chair! I don't know why Dad loves it so much, but he does." She shook her head and then gazed at him softly. "Fine. You are unnecessarily forgiven." Then she added, "For the record, you are welcome over here on my couch. On that side." She pointed to the cushion farthest away from her and smiled sweetly.

Finn laughed. "Point taken. I'm staying right here." He folded his arms in finality. He did get up to get their brownies, but after handing Allaya hers, he returned to the chair.

They spent the evening reliving many more memories about their summer adventures. Ally laughed so hard she cried as he described in more detail the events of his nude dash down the beach with his cousin, how he hadn't realized that his mother was on the beach that day, and that he'd spent the rest of the summer "offering" to clean the houses of all the women who had had the unfortunate chance to see his rear end flash across their picturesque afternoon.

"I still maintain that those women were lucky to get such a view, but my mom never saw it that way," he laughed.

They talked lightheartedly about Marielle and her germ-a-phobic tendencies; he shared his perspective of their sisterly fights and the scandalous kiss he'd shared with her oldest sister.

"I swear it was curiosity and nothing more. It was pretty lame," he admitted. "For starters there was no tongue, and I think we actually hit heads together before our lips ever met!"

He prodded gently into Ally's past two years of solitude. It didn't take her long to sum it up: she worked, ate when absolutely necessary, and came home to watch mindless TV or sleep until getting up the next morning to start the routine all over again. When he prodded her about her feelings during that time, she shrugged: "Empty. I just felt empty."

By the time nine o'clock rolled around, Finn was sitting on the floor leaning against the chair and she was on the couch cushion closest to him hugging her knees. They'd worn out every topic under the sun it seemed and they comfortably sat in silence.

"I never really realized how big a role you played in our lives," Allaya mused.

"I know. Me too."

"You were like our home away from home."

"Huh. That's an interesting way to put it."

"Well, the lake was always that for us, but I mean, without the people and the memories, this place would hold no value to me. Ya know?" she said thoughtfully.

"Yeah, I know exactly what you mean. That's how the school year was for me in some ways. Everyone I cared about returned home for the summer. But this was my home."

After a few more minutes of silence she spoke: "I'm sorry, Finn. I know that even before—during the school year—that we didn't keep in touch that often, but I'm especially sorry for afterwards. I didn't know what I was missing. Literally, *I missed so much.*" She hugged her knees tighter, her sprained ankle crossed over the uninjured one. "And not just you. I have a lot of apologies to make, but, you are here now, and . . . I'm sorry."

"Ally, we made a deal—"

"No Finn, really. I really need this. It's part of my process. I have to make the things right that I destroyed while I let myself be destroyed. I just need you to accept it and forgive me." She let out a deep breath and waited for his response.

Finn got up on his knees and inched over to the couch. He wrapped his hands around her good ankle and looked up at her, his eyes caring and soft.

"I accept it and forgive you," he said quietly. He leaned forward and kissed her knee.

"Thank you," she whispered, wiping the corner of her eyes.

He leaned his head against her knee and she ran her fingers slowly through his thick hair. Another comfortable silence passed between them. Allaya almost felt comforted by the ability simply to be in a room with another person. There was nothing hidden between the two of them, she didn't feel like she owed him anything, and she actually enjoyed the fact that he was with her probably more than she should have. She took a deep breath, trying to calm the nerves that were getting worked up inside her again.

"Hey, I have an almost harmless idea," Finn said suddenly, hoisting himself up from his knees. He disappeared into the kitchen and returned with two glasses of the wine they'd opened the day before and sat on the cushion opposite Allaya. Putting the glasses on the coffee table, he took the TV remote in his hands and started surfing the pay-per-view menu on the TV.

Allaya eyed him from her corner of the couch.

He highlighted an action movie and asked, "Is this all right?"

She nodded.

"Good. Now come here."

Warily, Ally scooted over toward Finn. He reached his arm out and pulled her into his side. Keeping his arm wrapped around her, he slid his hand under her arm.

"See? *Almost* harmless. I can handle it." He kissed the top of her head and settled into his place. He felt her body rise and fall in as she sighed. "Comfortable?"

"Yes," she said sincerely.

I'm more than comfortable. I can't believe how perfect it feels to be with him, she thought as the opening title sequence began to play.

About thirty minutes into the movie, Allaya shifted and slid down on the couch, so that her head was laying in Finn's lap. He moved his hand and absently ran his fingers through her hair. Allaya wasn't interested in the movie anymore. She closed her eyes and relished the gentle pressure of his fingers on her scalp.

She was almost asleep when Finn shifted slowly, lifting her head and rearranging himself to spoon her on the couch. With one arm under her head and the other wrapped securely around her waist, he settled deeply into the cushions of the couch.

"All good?" he asked.

"Mmmhmm." She put her hand on top of his and closed her eyes again; she felt his lips press softly against her ear and her stomach fluttered where his hand pressed against her belly. Suddenly she wasn't quite as sleepy anymore.

Finn felt her tense in his arms and immediately pulled his hand back to himself. "I'm sorry."

Allaya turned her head back and looked at him, her body shifting ever so slightly towards him. "So you're the one who's apologizing all the time now?" she asked softly.

"I don't want to push you."

"Then don't. Just kiss me." She turned her body the rest of the way to face his and drew his face to hers.

Finn sighed and gave in though what he felt was anything but defeat. He kissed her gently, slowly, careful to keep himself in check. He resisted the urge to sling his leg around hers and pull her closer. Allaya kept her hands pressed on his chest as if she might need to push him away at any given moment, but he didn't mind. She was kissing him back, that was what mattered.

Allaya wanted to slide her hands around his neck, to tangle her fingers in his hair, but she fought hard against the urge by gripping Finn's shirt so tightly in her fingers that her knuckles turned white.

A huge crash from the movie brought each of them back into the present, and they reluctantly pulled their lips away from each other's.

She sighed with her eyes closed. "You're right. That was totally your fault," she said with a smile.

"I take full responsibility." Finn kissed her forehead and then released his arm from behind her. Allaya turned her body and settled back in against him.

"Totally harmless," she scoffed.

"I said *almost* harmless! Almost!"

Allaya shook her head and pulled his arm back around her waist.

There were all sorts of things running through her brain as the fire inside of her began to wane and she started to doze again. What in the world could any of this be leading up to? There was a very inevitable separation looming before them in a few days, when they would both return to their respective realities. She didn't want to think about that, though; it had been so long since she'd felt comforted by anyone or anything. Even if her motives were slightly selfish, she wanted to enjoy the feeling while she could. She'd been disconnected for the past two years, and now here she was, feeling extremely connected. What would happen when they both left, in the opposite direction of each other? She finally silenced her thoughts and gave in to the rest that was beckoning her.

Allaya didn't stir when Finn tugged his arm out from underneath her and slid out from behind her. He had dozed off, too, but woke with a start around midnight. He was content to lay with her in his arms and watch her sleep, but after a few minutes, he knew it was in both of their best interests for him to at least move to the recliner, if not leave all together. He struggled for a moment over the decision, wishing that he possessed more self-control than he was feeling at the moment. Her hair framed her face and fell down around her neck. He had to resist the urge to run his fingers through it; he wanted nothing more than to move it out of the way and wake her with his kisses. He sighed and decided that he needed to go home, just to be on the safe side.

He stroked her cheek softly. "Ally," he whispered.

"Mmm?"

"I'm gonna head home alright? I'll call you in the morning?"

"Mmmhmm, that's fine."

"G'night, Ally."

"Mmmm."

He kissed her cheek, pulled a blanket around her and quietly left the cabin.

Allaya woke up early the next morning, the result of falling asleep so early the night before. She woke with a knot in her stomach, but it was not the fluttery, exciting knot she'd been experiencing for the past two days. This one was more like a reality knot. She had to go back to work in three days, and she had to leave the lake in two. Suddenly she felt a surge of pressure. What was she doing with Finn? Had she taken back enough ground to return to a normal life and to begin moving forward from where she left off before Marielle died? Or had she gotten in over her head and totally derailed herself? Would she suffer another heartbreak because of what she had allowed to transpire between herself and Finn? She rubbed her hands over her face in frustration while she made her way into the bathroom to get ready for whatever the day would throw at her.

"Ugh. God, I think I may have messed things up," she

groaned as she stared at her face in the bathroom mirror, all soapy from her cleanser. She sighed and wiped her face clean.

Finn had called; he was going to pick her up for lunch in a few hours. She had some time to herself, and for the first time since she got to the lake, she was actually dreading it. Even though the Father had spoken to her about her actions with Finn and blatantly told her that he was an important part of her life, she still felt as though she needed to be reprimanded or shamed for some of the thoughts she'd had about the man she was spending so much time with. But there was only silence.

With a deep breath, she grabbed her craft supplies, the small bucket of rocks she'd collected from the lake, and a pile of branches she'd set beside them, and headed to the back porch.

She sat on the rickety old picnic table staring at her small pile of stones, envisioning the project she had dreamed up. The day was mild, more overcast than anything else, but the birds were still flitting about her, the trees swaying in the breeze. Up the hill behind the house she watched some rabbits hop in and out of their nest. Life was going on all around her as she struggled to accept death.

She knew she was going to have to break her father's rule about the stones. She simply needed more than one per day. Arranging her stones this way and that, she tried to come up with the best plan of attack. Then an image suddenly came to her, and she started twisting and knotting branches. Once she had the basic idea, she began to stick the rocks in place with rubber cement. She was so focused on her project that she didn't hear Finn knock on the door a few hours later and let himself in.

"Hey! What're you doing?" his voice came out of nowhere.

Allaya nearly shot three feet in the air. "Holy crap, Finnigan! You scared the hell out of me!" Her hand flew to her chest.

"Whoa! Sorry! I knocked and called your name!"

She gasped for breath. "It's okay. Sorry."

He laid his hand on her back, in hopes of calming her. "So what are you up to? Is this the memorial thing?"

"Yeah. I just got the inspiration I needed and started putting it together."

"It looks great, Ally! I love it!" Finn exclaimed, running his fingers over the branches and stones that she was fashioning together.

"Thanks, I think it's going to turn out really good."

"Well, do you need more time or are you ready for lunch?"

"No, no. I'm good. We can go." She stood up and grabbed his arm quickly for support, wincing from the weight she'd put on her ankle.

He grinned. "I kinda like that you keep forgetting about that foot."

She blushed and started gathering up her supplies.

"I'll get that stuff." He gathered the haphazard collection into his hands and carried it inside through the backdoor.

"You can just lay it down by the door." Allaya indicated where she wanted it.

"I thought we could go into town and go to Dixie's. Is that okay?"

"Mmmm, Dixie's," she swooned. "Yes. Dixie's tomato soup is the best."

"Good. Let's go." He handed her the crutches and led

her out to his truck.

Dixie's Diner had been in town ever since Finn and Allaya were kids, and nothing had been changed or updated since it opened. The outside whitewashed paneled walls were badly in need of a paint job, and the porch needed to be fixed in a few places, as well as stained. Finn held the creaky door open for Allaya and then followed behind her. They sat in a booth by a window with sun-faded flowered curtains. Finn didn't pick up his menu right away. Instead, he watched Allaya's face as she skimmed over the menu that she had practically memorized years earlier. She noticed he was staring, and she smiled shyly.

"What?" She put down her menu, slouched forward, and rested her face on her hand.

"I was just thinking about what's next," he said, reaching for her free hand, lacing their fingers together.

"What's next?"

"Well, you know . . . Saturday . . . when you have to go back."

Her shoulders sagged. "Oh. Yeah. I've thinking about that this morning, too."

"I already told you. I'm not going anywhere."

"I know, Finn, but what does that really mean? Because, you are going somewhere. We both are! You're going home to work in Seattle, and I'm going back to Portland, to work and . . . to my family." The last word caused a lump in her throat that she struggled to swallow. She gazed down at their fingers, clasped together.

"I mean, I don't really know what we're doing here," she frowned. "Wow, that sounded awful. I didn't mean it to come out like that." She recognized the hurt that crossed his face and once again tried to swallow that lump in her throat. "I am enjoying this—enjoying you—but it's all just . . ."

"This is kind of fast, huh?" He rubbed his hand roughly across his face and pulled the other one from hers.

"Kind of." It was amazing to her that only hours ago she had felt so completely wrapped up in the euphoria of being close to him, of being kissed by him, and now there was a cold pit of uncertainty brewing in her gut. She felt as though she had only herself to blame for it, though. She'd allowed herself to get sidetracked. She seemed to forget about the fact that God himself had included Finn in the equation.

Finn sighed and looked out the window.

"I'll tell you what I know, Ally." He glanced back at her. She was still leaning toward him, ready to hear what he had to say.

"My mom called me last week. Last Monday," he said with emphasis. "She asked me if I would come and help her this week, and she said that you were going to be at the cabin." He paused again, watching her reaction. It didn't seem to register at first, and then she scrunched up her nose suddenly.

"But I didn't call her until Thursday!" She sat up straighter.

"I know."

"How did she . . . ?"

"I don't know. But when she said you were going to be here, it was like I didn't even have a choice. I just knew I had to come. I was being 'compelled,' like you said. So I came."

Allaya stared at him, confused.

"Do you think God told you to come?" She remembered

then that Finn had been in her dream and that she had gotten the impression in her heart that he was an important part of her process.

I don't understand what's going on! She leaned her head back against the booth and prayed for clarity.

"No. I'm not saying that. I'm just saying that, for some reason, I knew I had to be here." He reached for her hand again and said, "And I'm glad I came."

"I know, but it doesn't change the fact that I am leaving in two days. We've just opened up a huge can of . . . I don't even know what." She was at a loss for definition, "And I'm supposed to be focusing on reinventing my life or whatever and . . . I just . . ." She waved her hands in agitation, searching for words.

"Ally, slow down," Finn said, now reaching for the hand that was raised in midair.

She sighed and gave it to him; her eyes red-rimmed and her expression defeated.

"Listen, Ally, this is all as much of a surprise to me as it is to you. I didn't expect this. I really didn't. Even though there was nothing keeping me away from you this week, I still didn't come here planning to lose myself at the very sight of you."

"The very sight of me naked," she scoffed, rolling her eyes.

"No. Before that. At the dock." He leaned forward, his eyes locked on hers.

"What do you mean?"

"Ally, when I drove up to the lake and saw you laying on the dock, something ignited in me. I didn't recognize it then—I thought I was just happy after not seeing you for so long, happy to know that you were still alive! I mean, you were completely off the grid. Even Shara never mentions you."

"You talk to Shara?" she asked quietly, surprised.

"Yes, I still talk to Shara. We email occasionally. She's been really open about her struggle through all of this. I can't believe that I am the one to tell you this, but Ally, she's really changed. I mean, really. Have you talked to her at all lately?"

"No." She stared blankly at the table. Guilt was overwhelming her. She couldn't remember the last time she'd spoken one word to her sister.

"She almost never mentions you, but I know she misses you. Seriously, she's a different person."

She pulled her hands away and dragged them through her hair, overwhelmed. "Well, I am, too," she said defensively.

"I know. This changed everyone." He looked down sadly. "I'm sorry. I didn't mean to go there," he said apologetically. "Anyway, I pulled up to the dock and I was just, overcome by something. I was glad to see you. When you walked up to me, and I saw how miserable you looked, God, Ally . . ."

"Thanks a lot!" she rolled her eyes.

"I'm not kidding. Anyone who knows you would've seen the difference. But the last few days since we've been together, I've notice the color come back to your eyes. I'd say there's even a skip in your step, but . . ." he chuckled and eyed her crutches.

Allaya raised an eyebrow at him. "So you think you are to thank for the change?"

"I didn't mean that. What I mean is that I know you are going through your thing here, working out all that you need to. But Ally, you have changed something in me. I haven't seen or heard from you in over two years, and the past three days I have been completely consumed with you. I can't stop thinking about you. I can hardly keep my hands off you, and yet I have acted with more self-control than I've ever had to in my life."

The waitress came then, set down two glasses of water and looked at them expectantly.

"You ready?" she smacked her gum.

"Grilled cheese and tomato soup," Allaya said without looking up.

She could feel Finn's eyes on her. There was too much that she was trying to sort through. If she met his gaze, he would misinterpret what he saw. She was confused and hurting and trying to put up a wall to save herself from any more pain. All she really wanted to do was to get out of there. She needed a moment of silence to try to process what was going on inside her heart.

"I'll have a cheeseburger, well-done please," he said politely.

"Fries?"

"Uh, yeah. Thanks."

The waitress spun on her heel and disappeared through the swinging door at the end of the counter.

"Ally," he pried. "Allaya, what's wrong?"

"I just, I just don't know what to expect or what to do. I mean . . . this just came on so suddenly and there is so much I don't understand and so much that he is trying to tell me . . ." she trailed off.

"He?"

"Finn, you know." She gave him a serious look. "He is why I'm here, and even though you don't think so, I really think he's why you're here, too. Why your mom called you."

"I understand how important that is to you. I do. All of it."

"But what's important to you, Finn?" She finally looked up at him. She already knew what his answer would be. She knew that it would cause her heart to pound, but she also knew it wouldn't be the right answer.

"You," he stated simply.

They sat in silence for a while. He stared out the window, and she stared into the diner. He didn't understand what was happening. The past few days had been nothing short of amazing, and now it seemed she was turning the tables on him again. What had changed? Why was she shutting down again?

The waitress broke the silence a few moments later and set their plates and cutlery down with a clatter on the table.

Without glancing at him, Allaya picked up her spoon and started eating.

Twelve

They ate in silence. Well, Finn ate. Ally pushed her spoon around in her soup, only taking a few bites. When the waitress took their plates, Finn wiped his mouth with his napkin, set it down carefully and reached for Allaya's hand.

"Ally, I don't understand what's going on. What's changed?"

"I don't know, Finn. Something feels off," she sighed. She pulled her hand into her lap.

"What do you . . . I mean . . . what about the other day? On the dock? What about last night?"

"Those were quite possibly the most amazing moments ever," she smiled weakly.

"So then, what is wrong?"

"I don't know." Her eyes started to well up. "I want this," she gestured between the two of them, "whatever *this* is supposed to be. I want it, Finn. I want you. I just don't know if I can."

"Can what?"

She looked at him sadly. "It's too much, Finn." Tears spilled down her cheeks. She groaned and wiped them away with the back of her hand.

He sat back in surprise, "Wow."

"I'm sorry, Finn. I don't know how to do this—any of it! I don't know what God wants from me, I don't know what you want from me, or what I want!" A sob escaped her throat.

"Why are you so concerned with *him*, Ally? Why? What has *he* done for you? Huh? Isn't he the reason you're going through all of this anyway?" Finn growled.

She sat up sharply and looked at him, astonished. "Finn, don't!" she pleaded.

"Couldn't he have stopped this?"

"Finnigan. Stop!" She felt her throat close in panic.

"Couldn't he have saved her? What has he ever done for you?"

"STOP IT!" she cried out. She stood up, knocking over the crutches as she struggled her way out of the booth. She grabbed onto the table and limped towards the door as quickly as she could.

Finn slammed his fist into the table. He was completely unaware that the few patrons in the restaurant had witnessed the entire exchange and now sat frozen, staring at him. He shook his head as he watched Ally stumbling towards the truck. He angrily threw some cash on the table, grabbed her crutches and walked out, trying to calm himself down.

He had crossed the line. He knew it. Who was he to ask her those kinds of questions? Who was he to accuse her God of murdering her sister? He'd just ruined everything. If he could've taken himself out back and beaten the crap out of himself, he would have. Instead, he walked over to where Ally was fumbling with the door handle and closed his hand over hers.

"Ally," he said softly.

She ignored him, pushed his hand away and finally got the door open.

"Ally, I'm so sorry. I was wrong. I shouldn't have said those things."

She pulled herself into the seat and stared straight ahead.

"Ally, please. I just don't understand what in the hell is going on here. One minute we are connecting on this level together. Like you said, the most amaz—"

She interrupted him. "Can you please drive me back?" She wiped at her eyes.

"Ally, listen."

"Finnigan, please drive me back to the cabin or so help me I will walk," she glared at him.

Swearing, he slammed her door shut and stalked around to the driver's side. He peeled out of the parking lot and back in the direction of the lake.

She stared out the window, sobbing quietly the entire drive back to the cabin and his angry questions played over and over in her mind. She just needed to be alone. She needed to yell and scream. Finn couldn't possibly have known that the questions he threw out in accusation were the very questions she had been trying so hard to ignore. She was too scared of being disowned. Too scared that God would be angry with her for how she really felt about Marielle's death. God *could* have stopped it. He *could* have saved her. So why didn't he? Finn was lost in his own angry thoughts on the other side of the truck: *Is this part of your amazing plan? Dangling her in front of me? Taunting me?* "Look here

Finn, look what I've got that you can't have." Why in the world do you deserve such dedication from her? You ruined her.

He was seething. She had been within his reach. He had had a grasp on her, and suddenly, without warning, she was gone. She was right. It was all too much. Way too much. If he'd just kept his damned mouth shut. He pulled up to the cabin and started to get out to help her.

"I can manage," she said and slid out of her seat. Slamming the door shut, she slowly made her way up the path. She stumbled at the stairs, and he ran towards her. She let him help her up the stairs, but once at the door, she swatted him away. He grabbed her arm roughly, though, and pulled her to him.

"Ally, I'm sorry," he said and kissed her firmly on the mouth, a last ditch effort to try to salvage the feelings between them.

She struggled to get out of his grip, but he held her tightly and she couldn't help but succumb to his kiss, defenseless and broken. Her heart was torn between wanting to push him away and wanting to pull him closer at the same time.

He slipped his arms around her waist and pressed harder against her, deepening the kiss, unwilling to let it end.

Allaya clenched his hair in her fingers; she could feel fresh tears on her cheeks as she kissed him back.

If I can just keep her here, he thought. *If I can just remind her of how good this could be . . .*

"Stop. Finn, stop," she pushed him away, and when he wouldn't let her go, she pounded on his chest with her fists. "You have to go. Please. Please go. Let me go." She turned her face away as he tried to kiss her again.

"Please," she whispered and gave one final push. He released her, and she stumbled back, falling into the door. He reached to catch her but she pushed him away again. "No! Leave, Finn. Go!" She quickly let herself into the cabin and shut the door firmly behind her.

Finn slumped against the railing of the first step of the porch, defeated. Her tears were still wet on his face. He sniffled and wiped them off, only to feel his cheeks dampening again.

What the hell? He realized that he was the one crying this time. That made him angry. He stormed off to the truck, once again slamming the door behind him and roaring away from the cabin.

Allaya had barely made it in the door before she collapsed on the floor with gut wrenching sobs. She heard the truck tear off and that only made her cry harder.

"What are you doing to me?" she cried out.

Restoring.

She remained on the floor for hours, weeping, begging answers of her God. Though his voice was silent, she could feel the areas of her heart that she had hidden from him begin to unfold like a flower in the sun. She gathered up all the strength she could muster and crawled through the cabin on her knees, wiping her nose as she went, until she reached the door that she hadn't been able to enter yet. She stretched out a trembling hand and turned the knob, pushing the door open. She continued to crawl into the middle of the room, where she lay down, pulling her knees into her chest.

"Jesus," she whispered as she lay on her side, weary and emotionally spent, in the middle of the room that the three girls shared during their summers at the lake. It was the first time she had been in there in two years. The bunk beds were in front of her against the wall, and Shara's single bed beside her. The sun was shining through the window, directly on the spot where she lay on her side, her hands limp on the floor.

"I don't understand!" she whispered. "I know this is always going to hurt. I know she will never come back, and I will always miss her. But I am mad," she hiccupped, "at you!"

The tears continued to roll quickly across the bridge of her nose and down her cheeks onto the musty rug underneath her. She drew in a ragged breath.

"I don't want to be mad, but I am!" her voice gradually grew louder than a whisper. "I don't understand. Why did you do this? Why did you take her?"

Sobs ravaged her body as she finally admitted what had held her captive for the past two years. Yes, there had been the insurmountable grief, but with it had come a thief in the night—a thief who had told her that the God she believed in was powerless, heartless, and cruel.

"I know bad things happen, and I know that it must break your heart to see your people in pain. So why do you let it happen? Not just death, like Marielle's, but sickness and pain and suffering. You can stop it! Why don't you stop it? I don't understand!" She pulled herself up to a kneeling position, anchoring her arms to the floor in support of her upper body as she yelled into the room.

The answers aren't easy Allaya, and they won't change anything. What needs to take over your questions and take root in your heart is that I am good. And that is my word.

"I don't know if I can ever trust you and your word again!

You took her! You take all the time!" she shouted into the air. "You didn't save her! Why didn't you save her?"

Allaya's face pressed against her hands on the ground. The sounds originating in her gut were almost animal-like as the pain and doubt ripped through her like a tidal wave. She posed the questions she was most afraid of having answered. She was sure she wouldn't come out of this conversation alive. How could she accuse God of anything?

"You didn't save her!" she whispered.

I did. I did save her, sweetheart. That's why she's here now, with me. Because I saved her.

Allaya sat up abruptly, agony and confusion flooded her heart as she looked around the room, as if she were looking for him to show himself in human form. A whimper escaped her mouth and she clutched her fingers to heart, where the pain was like fire burning her from the inside out.

Her death was not a loss, Allaya. Her death was not a score for the other team. Her death was my victory.

"It's a loss for me!" she cried softly. She felt defeated and worn out. She felt her lungs constricting as she fought to control her ragged breathing.

I know, my love, and I know you are broken. I want nothing more than to heal you and restore your heart. But if you look, you will see—nothing I have done is without purpose. Everything that comes from my hand has value, and purpose, and is intended for your abundant life.

Allaya was incredulous. "Is that supposed to make me feel better?" she scoffed and sat back on her legs, wincing at the pain in her ankle but feeling as though she probably deserved the feeling. "You want what's best for me so you kill my sister?

Seriously? God, WHO *ARE* YOU?" She flung her hands out from her sides in desperate questioning.

I am your Father. The lover of your wounded soul. But Allaya, it is not you that I answer to. But you that answer to me, and Marielle answered to me as well. When she went to Africa, she answered to me. When her life ended, she answered to me.

Allaya's stomach dropped as the weight of the truth sunk in. She pulled her hands back in and buried her face in them.

"Oh God!" she cried. "God no! I'm sorry! I'm so sorry!" She wanted to take back all of her accusations and just go back to the way things had been. She second-guessed coming to the lake, tackling this huge tear in her heart. She didn't want to go any farther. She didn't want to hear anymore. But the voice she had asked to speak kept revealing truth in her heart.

I found her worthy Allaya. I found her just and good and faithful. I found her precious and perfect. She is more valuable to me than gold. I didn't allow this in order to hurt you Allaya; I'm not punishing you for something. I know that's what you think. I know that your doubt has made you feel unacceptable and that your fear of me has kept you locked away from everyone you love. I know the lies that the enemy has told you about me, and believe me, his day of reckoning is coming.

Hear the truth, Allaya: You are more valuable to me than anything. That's never changed. You don't have to be afraid of me. I know the state of your heart and I love you, Allaya, no matter what. You are my favorite child. My most prized possession. Nothing will change that. Marielle's absence from your life isn't something you could have done

anything about. There is nothing you could have done to change what happened. You couldn't have loved her more; you couldn't have done anything different that would have changed the outcome of her decisions. But I was there with her through the very end. I carried her out of that place of darkness. I alone am good. That is my promise to you. I never fail.**

Allaya's face contorted as though in physical pain and her tears streamed faster down her cheeks.

I am good.

She leaned forward, clutching at her chest again, shoulders shaking as she let the Father begin to move inside her spirit.

I am good.

The words washed over her body from head to toe, yet she knew the work was not yet finished. She still blamed him.

I am good.

By now she was prostrate on the floor. He continued to speak over her until she finally released herself from the anger, the blame she'd cast on God, and the seeping wounds of her heart.

I am good.

"I know," she whispered.

You know, but do you *believe*?

"I believe."

Do you trust me?

"I . . ." she stumbled over the words, "I trust you." She closed her eyes as a new wave of tears poured out of her lids and exhaustion overcame her. She curled up on her side and fell asleep, feeling physically cradled in the arms of her Savior, and while she slept, he began to stitch her heart back together, gently and with a thread that could not be broken.

I love you, my sweet. I love you. I love you. I love you.

Finn didn't make it far down the highway before his rage and tears blinded him. He pulled off to the side of the road and beat his head against his steering wheel.

He began to scream things into the air that would have made his mother slap him.

You can curse me as much as you want or we can talk. It's your choice. I'll be here no matter what.

"You know what? I don't need this. I don't need her, and I sure as hell don't need you." He practically spat the words out of his mouth and reached to start the ignition, pushing the overwhelming thoughts out of his head.

You're wrong.

Finn growled and shoved the truck into drive and veered back onto the highway, imagining a person left standing where he once sat, staring after him, wounded and abandoned.

Carolyn was already in bed when she heard Finn slam the door in the mudroom. She started to get up, but something stopped her. Instead, she lay still and listened as her son banged around the kitchen. He was cursing and muttering.

He never listens, she thought to herself sadly. There was only one reason why he could be so upset right now. She'd warned him to keep himself in check. But she was sensitive to what was going on, to what needed to happen. She assumed that he was just merely thinking with . . .well, among other things, his head and not his heart, and not the spirit that lay dormant inside of him.

Oh, Lord, what have we done?

I am working on them. Go work on him. He needs you.

She heard cupboards slamming and he swore again, louder. Carolyn reached for her robe and stepped quietly into the kitchen. On the counter were all the fixings for a sandwich, minus the bread.

"Sweetheart?" she said cautiously.

He jumped at the sound of her voice anyway. "Geez, Mom!"

"Sorry dear. What do you need?"

Finn crossed his arms and looked down, frustrated. "I can't find the bread."

"We're out. The truck comes tomorrow. There are some hamburger buns in the pantry if you'd like." She walked to the pantry and pulled out the buns.

"Thanks," he sighed.

"Do you want to talk?"

"No."

"All right. Coffee?"

"No."

"Beer?"

"Yes."

Carolyn smiled softly and pulled two bottles out of the fridge. Twisting the caps off both, she pulled up a stool and sat down. It was silent for a few minutes before Finn opened up.

"Mom, why did you call me out here?" He slumped forward on the counter, head hanging.

"What do you mean?"

"Why did you call me to tell me that Ally was coming?"

"Do you really want to know?"

"Yes." He looked expectantly at his mother.

"Well honey, you're not going to like it."

"Mom, tell me."

She shrugged. "I had been talking and praying on the phone with Audrey Sheldon about Allaya for months. They were so concerned about where she was headed, or, I suppose, not headed. She hadn't spoken with them in ages. Anyway, Audrey asked me to check on something in the house; there was a letter from the water company or something and she needed some information. So as I was getting the papers from the house, I was praying for Allaya, and the Lord told me very plainly that she was going to be coming to the lake and so I began to pray more. And Finn, even though I was praying for her with all my heart, I couldn't get you out of my mind. For whatever reason, the Father wanted you to be here while she was here. He didn't tell me why, just that I had to tell you, and that he would take care of the rest. He did, because you're here and so is she." She took a long sip of her beer.

"He did a *great* job," Finn said sarcastically while taking a long swig from his bottle.

Carolyn looked at him quizzically.

"I did something stupid, Mom. I did what you told me not to do, and I stuck my nose where it didn't belong. I think I made it worse for her. I definitely made it worse for me."

"What happened, Finn?"

He recounted the scene from the diner and ended with simply leaving in his truck and heading home.

"You came straight home?" Carolyn looked at the clock that read 10:15 p.m.

"Well, no . . ." he trailed off. Setting his beer down, he sunk his head into his hands, leaning against the countertop.

Carolyn waited.

Finally he groaned and said, "Ever since I got here, ever since I saw Ally, God . . ." he groaned again, "God has been talking to me."

Carolyn's eyes pricked with tears and she pressed her lips together, struggling to compose herself. It didn't surprise her that God had spoken, but knowing for sure that her son could still hear him when he spoke was a treasure.

"What has he said?"

"Stuff that you would say," he muttered, rolling his eyes.

Carolyn chuckled and set her beer down, reaching for Finn's hand.

"What has he said?" she asked again.

"A lot, surprisingly, because I've had nothing to say to him for years."

He knew that wouldn't be enough for her, so he went on. "He said basically, that if I didn't accept him, then I could never have her or that she wouldn't have me. He said to wait, to slow down. Then tonight, well, I was angry, Mom. Everything I said, I said because I was angry. I still am. This whole 'God' thing just doesn't make sense to me when I look at things like Marielle, or Dad, or anything bad in the world. How could a 'good God' let those things happen?"

"Oh, Finn," Carolyn sighed. "First of all, your father made choices that lead to his death. He was well aware of the risks involved in his habits, as was I. We both, I suppose, just thought he could continue on, flying under the radar of consequence. Even when he was diagnosed, he couldn't give up his cigarettes. He'd smoked for years and years, and I didn't stop him. His death was entirely about the choices that he made."

"But, Mom, he was a good man! He went to church, he gave his money to the poor, he loved God."

"Yes, honey, and he is with Jesus now because he loved and served the Lord. But those things don't change the fact that he willfully poisoned his own body every day, almost every hour!"

"So, then what about Marielle?"

"That one is a bit more difficult for even me to understand. But, hang on." Carolyn got up and left the kitchen, returning a few moments later with her old, worn leather Bible.

Finn sighed at the sight of it.

"Give me a chance, dear. Hold on." She thumbed through the pages carefully. The crinkle of the pages stirred a sense of peace in Finn. He remembered when he was little, the hours that his mother would sit in her chair, reading the Bible quietly or sometimes aloud to him. He had loved the sound the thin pages made as she carefully turned them.

"Here we go," she said, "'For whoever wants to save his life will lose it, but whoever loses his life for me and for the gospel will save it,' Mark 8:35."

"I don't get it."

"Well, baby, it's not necessarily talking about dying physically here. When I think of this verse and I think of Marielle and the sacrifice that she made— willingly, keep in mind, because again she knew the dangers involved, the risks that she would be taking, but she still chose to go. So I have some peace about it all. I would much rather that she were still alive and that she were here with us, healthy and youthful as she always was," Carolyn brushed a tear away, "but I know where she is now, and trust me Finn, she is so much better off. Nothing can harm her now, and her Father is rejoicing in her and in the sacrifice she made so that others could know him. She lost her life for the sake of the gospel. For the sake of sweet innocent little boys and girls, and mothers and fathers in Africa who had no other way of hearing about the love of the Father. She gave that to them. That is huge."

"I don't know, Mom. I don't know if I can swallow all that."

Carolyn sighed. "I know. It's not an easy thing to deal with. We feel such a loss, even though she is in complete victory."

Finn stared as his mother, lacking understanding. He needed an easy answer, but that didn't seem to be available.

"As far as Ally goes, honey, like I said, give it time. You provoked a lot in her tonight, and she is wrestling with so much right now. You've got to give it time."

"I know. I'm such an idiot."

She put her hand over his. "No, you're not, Finn. You got emotional. It's going to be okay. It won't be the last time!"

"But of all the insensitive, uncaring things to say . . ."

"How do you know it wasn't just what she needed to hear? That it wasn't what broke down that last barrier between her and the other side of this whole thing? You just never know, Finn." She downed the last of her beer and threw it in the recycling bin.

"Ask him, honey. Ask the Father what the next step is."

"Mom, I—"

"I know you don't want to, but if you really want her, you've got to give him a chance." She walked over and reached up to kiss his cheek. "I love you," she whispered, caressing his face. Then she turned on her heel back to her bedroom.

Finn folded his arms and slumped against the cabinets. "I can't do this tonight," he said to the empty kitchen.

I'm not going anywhere.

Thirteen

Finn went to bed trying to turn off his thoughts. They meandered around for a while, but eventually they stopped on his own father.

Steven Meyers had been an abrupt man. He had never wasted time on details or explanations. He simply moved forward, all the time. He and Finn's relationship had been distant at best, and Finn tried endlessly as a child to gain his father's attention. The only instances that really caused Steven to stop and see his child were the ones that ended in some form of discipline. Carolyn would encourage them both individually to seek the other out, and it hurt her heart to watch her son grow up without any kind of connection to his own dad. But Steven was not one to give way to emotions. He and Finn would go fishing on the lake and Finn would help around the cabins and at the store, and all the while Finn would simply be looking for a word of appreciation, pride or encouragement. Everything they did together was much more about the process than the time spent.

It appeared to Finn that the two most important things in his father's life were his mother and God, in that order. Still, Finn never stopped trying to win a spot of his own.

When his father was diagnosed with cancer, things changed a little. While he never once gave up a single cigarette, his heart seemed to soften a little and he began to take more care with his time. He extended invitations to Finn, especially while in his last days, to come and sit in the room with him. It wasn't amazing, but it was more than his father had ever given to him before.

They talked about the upkeep of the store and the homes on the lake; they made plans to repair this dock or that fence. It was as much as Steven could give, and he knew full well that he'd already wasted the time he'd been given. Finn knew if they could just have a second chance that they could be the father and son he'd always dreamed of. He prayed and prayed and prayed, asking God for a miracle even if it was just a simple show of affection from his dad.

Then one day, when Finn woke up, he knew that it was all over. He could hear his mother talking to someone on the phone. She was crying—there had been a lot of crying, but that time was different. There was ache communicated through her sobs—not fear, but absolute desperation. He got up slowly and peered out of his bedroom door and jumped back as he saw paramedics coming toward him, wheeling a gurney down the hall. There was a body on it, covered in a sheet. He remembered staring after them, feelings jumbled, unsure how to respond. After his mom ended her call, she tapped on his door.

"Oh, Finn," she whispered when he opened it, grabbing a hold of him. Then frantically she yelled, "Wait!!! WAIT!" and ran after the paramedics. She stopped them on the walk. "Please, my son needs to say goodbye." She walked back in the house and grabbed Finn's hand. "Come on, honey."

"Mom, I don't wa—" Finn remembered how sick to his stomach he had felt at the thought of seeing the deceased body of his father.

"I know, love, but if you don't, you will always regret it. You have to say goodbye."

"Mom, no," he protested.

"Finn, I'm not going to force you, but I'm asking you to do this. Please."

Finn sighed and let go of his mother's hand, starting toward the spot where the paramedics were waiting to load the gurney into the ambulance.

They pulled the sheet down and Finn stared at his father.

Finn remembered it like it had just happened, as if it were happening all over again. His father looked as though he were merely sleeping but for the slight bluing of his lips. The disease had weakened him months before; his skin hung loosely around his cheekbones and jaw.

Finn stood silently for a minute. He wasn't sure what to do. He wanted to run away and never turn back, to scream and break things. But he stood in the moment, totally paralyzed, with that sick feeling twisting in his stomach.

Finally, he muttered the words, "Bye, Dad."

He turned on his heel and walked back to the house, where he locked himself in his room for the rest of the day, tuning out visitors and sympathizers with rock music blasting through his headphones.

It was soon after Steven's funeral that Finn decided he

was done with God, who had completely ignored his requests for a miracle. He was done with caring about what people thought or how they felt, done with letting anyone close enough to fail him. He had managed to hold out on those convictions for a long time, until the past few days he had spent with Allaya. How was it possible? He had spent thirteen years building walls around himself—letting no one within firing range—and in a record one hour, all of his defenses had been shattered to the ground. How could it be?

Finn rolled over and stared out the window. The moon shone brightly into his room, casting a shadow of the windowpane across his bed. He might never know the answers to his questions now. He had done irreparable damage. He had taken all of his own anger and blame out on Allaya, and he knew that there was no way he could take any of it back. He fell asleep cursing himself.

At some point during the night, Allaya had crawled to one of the beds in the room and climbed in. She woke up in the morning and took in her surroundings, a little disoriented. She was in the single bed—in Shara's bed.

Shara. The feeling that wrapped around her heart surprised Allaya. *I miss her.*

She sat up and rubbed her eyes. She kept the trauma of the previous day from her thoughts and chose to dwell on the promises the Father had spoken to her through the night.

To further convince herself, she said, "You are good," out loud with her hands pressing on her heart. She took a deep breath and swung her legs off the bed, gingerly stepping on her twisted ankle. The pain was considerably less, and she managed to make it to the bathroom to turn on the shower with ease. She peeled off the day-old clothes and stepped into the shower, already full of steam. The heaviness that had made its home on top of her heart for so long was lifting, and she hummed a little while she bathed. It felt good to be able to breathe again without feeling like there was a brick on her chest.

It was an effort to keep Finn out of her mind, but she continued to squash those thoughts with plans for the day. She needed a few more stones for her project, so, even though the rule was one rock per day, she was going to have to get a few more than that. She only had until the next afternoon. There was still work to be done before she could finish affixing the stones to her project, though, so after she toweled off and put on a fresh pair of shorts and a T-shirt, she grabbed her supplies again and opened the back door.

She paused for a moment to breathe in her surroundings. A slight breeze caressed the branches of the huge pine trees that hovered overhead, rustling the needles. The fragrance of the woods brought back memories like a slide show in her mind. Allaya closed her eyes and reveled in the scenes as they played out. She smiled as she remembered playing hide-and-seek with her father and sisters when they were little, roasting hot dogs around the fire pit, and later getting all gooey from the marshmallows they had burned. She remembered sitting outside with Marielle, examining their rocks while Shara sat on the porch reading. She remembered stumbling upon Finn and Shara behind the big rock up the hill.

Allaya stood up taller and opened her eyes, squashing Finn down deep inside her vat of memories again. "There is just too much else going on," she said to herself, and she set to work on her project.

Unsure of how long she had been working, Allaya was startled when she heard the sound of a car pulling up to the cabin. Her first thought of who it could be made her heart stop for more reasons than she cared to admit, but she quickly decided that the motor wasn't loud enough to be a truck. She walked around the side of the porch and saw a familiar silver sedan sitting in the driveway and a head full of chocolate brown curls.

"Mom," she whispered, and she willed herself not to spill any more tears.

Allaya hurried through the back door of the cabin to meet her mother at the front. She threw open the door just as Audrey was about to knock.

"Allaya, I—" she looked as though she should be punished, like a dog caught messing in the trash. In spite of the dark circles under her eyes, she was still as beautiful as ever: her green eyes glistened with tears and soft brown curls framed her rouge-dusted cheeks.

"Mom!" Allaya threw her arms around her mother and held her tight. Nervously her mother returned the hug, and soon it was a bone-crushing grip. Allaya felt her mother shaking in her arms.

"Laya! Oh Laya!" her mother sobbed. Allaya breathed in the familiar scent of lavender and honey, which was her mother's signature perfume. It was like antibiotics to Allaya's healing heart.

Audrey pulled away from her daughter and wiped her eyes. "I'm sorry, honey. I shouldn't have barged in."

"Mom, no. I'm sorry. I'm *so* sorry." Allaya's eyes shone in the sun.

"Oh, sweetheart!" she cried and pulled her daughter to her again.

Allaya felt like the puzzle pieces of her heart were being put back into place, that she was almost complete. Almost.

Audrey took a step back, looking her daughter over from head to toe. "You're too skinny!" she said abruptly.

Allaya laughed and pulled her toward the door. "Then you should cook for me!"

"Still smells the same." Audrey glanced around the cabin wistfully, years worth of memories crossing her face in a single second. "Wow. This is the first time I've been here since . . ." she trailed off.

"I know." Allaya linked arms with her mother and stared into the cabin. "I'm starving," she suddenly realized. "Let me make you a sandwich."

A short while later, settled across the table from Allaya with a turkey sandwich, Audrey felt the need to explain herself.

"I'm sorry to barge in on you, sweetheart. I just . . . I just couldn't hold myself back any longer. It has been torture. Absolute torture."

Allaya set her sandwich down and grabbed her mother's hand. "It's been torture on this side, too, Mom. I am so sorry."

"Laya, you don't have to—"

"Yes, Mom, I do. I am sorry that I pulled away from you all. I had no capacity for dealing with what happened. I had no playbook to tell me how I should respond or feel, and it was so much easier to be numb and shut down, or, at least, I thought it was easier. I suppose it just prolonged the inevitable, but, Mom, I love you, and I should never have cut myself off. I can see now how much doing that caused death in my own heart."

She took a deep breath, willing away tears, before continuing. "I have ached for you guys, but I couldn't bring myself to reach out. I am so sorry for causing even more pain for you, Dad, and Shara, too." A tear slipped down her cheek and she took another deep breath.

Audrey got up and moved to the chair beside Allaya.

"There are no adequate words to express what we have experienced. No one should ever have to experience loss like this—or of any kind, for that matter. But we're still here. We're still fighting. We are still a family—broken, maybe—but we are still a family. You are still my baby girl." Audrey ran her fingers through her daughter's hair. "I have missed you so much."

"Mom, this week has been so hard. So painful. I have had to wrestle with so much. I have had to admit and confess so much to Jesus. I never thought I could have a real conversation with him again. I thought that after the things I said to him, he would never love me again. But he never left me." She faced her mother. "I didn't hold back, even though I thought for sure I would die on the spot for speaking some of those things out loud. But he was so gentle with me. He was so good to me. He is good, and all I can do is cling to that when I start to hurt and to question. I know I still have a long ways to go, but Mom, I'm going to be okay. I'm ready to come home."

Audrey's tears poured down her cheeks and she grabbed hold of her daughter with a death grip. "I'm not going to let you go again." she shook her head. "I'm going to fight harder for you than ever!"

Allaya relaxed in her mother's arms, letting the safety of that embrace fill the void that had been empty for so long. "I don't think it will ever stop hurting, though, Mom. I don't think

I'll ever stop missing her."

"I don't expect it will." Audrey sat up and pulled Allaya far enough away to look in her eyes. "There are still nights that I cry myself to sleep," she admitted. "I'm sure there will always be those nights. She's not here anymore, and nothing is going to change that. Of course, we will always miss her," she brushed a tear from under Allaya's eye, "that can only be expected."

Allaya nodded and picked up her sandwich again.

After they finished their lunch, Allaya took her mom outside to show her the project she'd been working on. On the patio table lay two small bundles of branches, twisted and tied together to form a cross. The stones that Allaya had been collecting were cemented carefully in various places on the cross. There were still a lot of empty spots that needed rocks, but the general idea came across.

Audrey gasped, "Laya! It's beautiful! Oh my goodness! It's absolutely perfect," she exclaimed.

"I was going to enclose it in a glass box or frame or something and bring it home to you and Dad."

"Sweetheart, this is absolutely priceless. It is going to mean so much to him, to all of us! You are brilliant!" Audrey kissed Allaya on the cheek.

"Well, I need more stones, though. I was going to head down to the lake this afternoon to get the rest. I have to break Daddy's rule, but I figured it would be all right, just this once." She ran her fingers over the stones softly.

"I'll help, and we won't tell him." Audrey smiled at her daughter. She felt a hope rise in her heart that she hadn't felt in years. At least one of her daughters was back.

Hours later, the two women lay on their towels on the dock, the sun drying the water droplets left on their skin from their expedition to the bottom of the lake. The bucket they'd brought down from the cabin was full of rocks—more than enough to finish Marielle's cross. There was no sound but the chirping of birds and the occasional splash of a fish in the lake. Allaya imagined that the water left on her skin was like the last remaining residue from her pain and darkness and that as the sun dried each drop, it also erased the residue. She didn't just feel like herself again, she was herself, perhaps a better version even. It was okay to smile, to be noticed, and to feel. There was just one drop the sun couldn't seem to erase.

"Have you seen Finn?" her mother asked suddenly, as if reading her mind.

Allaya stiffened. There it was. The new pain. She sat up and spun on her rear end toward her mother. Audrey was propped up on her elbows looking at her.

Allaya let out a breath. "Yes," her voice cracked.

Come on. Get over it. He's just a distraction, and I'm headed in a good direction. Let it go, she told herself.

Don't let go. The Lord's voice permeated her thoughts yet again.

"UUUUUGH!" Allaya grunted.

"What? What is it?"

"I am so sick of crying!" she shouted, slumping her head into her hands. She heard the dock creak as her mother moved over to her and put her hand on her knee.

"Laya, what's wrong?"

Allaya sniffled and said something unintelligible.

"Honey? What?"

"I love him, Mom."

"Who? Finn? You love Finn?" The surprise in Audrey's voice was obvious.

"Yes."

"What?" Audrey gasped.

"I know, Mom. I know. It's only been a few days, and he's a jerk, except that he's really not, and," she groaned, "Mom, he's been here. I mean, not just 'here' here, but he's *been* with me." The words spilled out of her mouth faster than she could register the thoughts. "He has helped me so much this week, and somewhere—totally out of left field—there was a current to his touch, like it was electric, and suddenly, while I was still trying to figure out how I was going to recover from everything, he became a part of the equation, and . . ." She was breathless as she stammered on. "I think I love him, and it doesn't make any sense. At all!"

Audrey was speechless. She certainly hadn't expected this. Her girls had befriended Finn when they were children, and, aside from the one incident with Shara, Audrey had never given him a second thought in that regard. He'd become like an adopted part of their family during the summertime, which naturally resulted in the close relationship between herself and his mother. She looked into her daughter's face and saw The Look—the tortured look of a girl helplessly in love.

"What about the . . . uh . . . 'jerk' part?" she asked, sounding a little more than confused.

"It's a long story. I suppose I should actually thank him for what he said. He was more honest with me than I could have ever been with myself." Allaya trailed off as the pieces fit together in her head.

"Honey, you're going to have to start from the beginning. You're losing me."

Allaya recounted the week's events to her mother, sparing little detail. She did leave out the part about the night of the storm but flowed freely with the rest. She ended with their argument in the diner, and then with how she had pushed him away on the steps of the cabin.

"That is what really broke me. I mean, that's what really got me on my face, finally screaming my accusations, finally throwing my confusion and questions in the Lord's face. Finn's rant showed me how I really felt about it all. Wow," she said slowly, as if a light bulb had turned on in her head.

"But," she continued, "the difference is that I took my questions and feelings, and I confronted the Lord about it. Finn won't do that, and I can't force him to. I can't be God to him. I can't change him."

"Whoa, Laya. Just, whoa. I never ever dreamed this would happen. And you said that the Lord said that Finn was to be a part of this? Of your healing?"

"Well, he basically said that Finn is as much a part of this as he wants to be. It's up to Finn, I guess."

"So then, you have to wait," Audrey said as if it were the obvious answer.

"Wait?"

"Yes, honey! God is doing something in Finn—something important. I think this week was just as important for him as it was for you. For completely different reasons and then also for the same one. You two are involved in each other's stories somehow, and right now, your job is to wait and pray."

"Mom, I don't know if I can." Allaya hung her head again

and her shoulders began to tremble.

Audrey took her hand and cupped Allaya's chin, turning her face back up. "You can, honey. If you really do love him, then you have to. You have to let it go and trust that the Father has Finn taken care of. You've got to be able to continue with your life now. Don't let this stunt the growth that has begun here. There is a reason for all of this, and when the work is done the Father will show you what it is. Sweetheart, he has such good gifts for you."

"Yeah," Allaya said dryly. "I've heard that somewhere before." She sniffled and rubbed the back of her hand across her nose. "Gosh. It's like I've traded one nightmare for another."

Audrey chuckled and said, "It would seem that way, but this could turn out to be a fantastic reality, honey. Absolutely beautiful." Audrey's expression turned a little dreamy as she closed her eyes and looked toward the sun. She looked back at her daughter with an amused expression on her face. "Finn Meyers? Scrawny, gangly, kissed-your-sister Finn Meyers?"

"Yeah. I know." Allaya rolled her eyes and leaned into her mom. "You should see him now though," she sighed helplessly.

"Well, well. The Father sure loves to surprise us," Audrey grinned and squeezed Allaya.

Fourteen

Finn packed up the small duffel he had brought to the lake, kissed his mother goodbye despite her pleas for him to stay, climbed in his truck, and turned the wheel toward the highway back to Seattle. He had felt so compelled to be at the lake that week and for what? Some carnal pleasure? Just a glimpse of what he could have, only to have the door slammed in his face?

I don't need to leave home to experience that. One phone call to Tanya and . . . he stopped himself mid-thought, realizing that dealing with Tanya might be worse than what he was struggling with now. He cranked up the radio and imagined the voice that had been plaguing him fading in the distance—along with the lake, his mother's home, and all of the events of the last few days.

"I can't hear you," he said out loud for effect.

Silence.

"Perfect." He focused himself on the songs playing on the radio, and two hours later he pulled his truck into the driveway of his workshop.

He felt the need to sweat, to use his power to make something do what he wanted it to do. He needed creative freedom. His client orders would have to wait. Finn unloaded the huge log from his truck and positioned it on his workbench. He had already stripped off the bark at the lake and now he used his saw to cut it into two pieces, and then he smoothed the ends. He hoisted one of the pieces up onto the table saw and carefully ran it through, splitting it clean down the middle. As the log split across the table, he noticed a discoloration in the wood. He pulled out his knife and pushed it into the wood. It went trough with barely any effort.

"No, no!" he cursed. When Finn twisted the knife around a little, the inner part of the log began to crumble. It was rotting from the inside out.

"Shit." He shoved that piece on the floor and grabbed the other half of it. Same thing. All four quarters of the tree were affected by rot.

Finn got angry and threw down his knife in the dirt. He wiped the back of his hand across his forehead and looked up at the clock. He'd barely been there an hour, but already he was hungry and tired. He shoved the logs aside with his feet, locked the shop and drove ten minutes to get home.

He half expected Tanya to be waiting for him in the apartment, but she wasn't. There was an envelope on the floor in front of the door when he walked in. It was creased from being shoved under the door and inside it were his spare key and a note that read, "I have a dream, too" in Tanya's messy script. Finn sighed and tossed the key onto the coffee table. He crumpled the note and threw it away.

"Good for you, Tanya. Go dream about someone who

won't ruin your life." He pulled a beer from the fridge and snapped the lid across the room. It hit the blinds on the window. He grabbed the last slice of pizza from a box in the fridge and slumped down on the couch, flipping on the TV without much interest in what was playing.

Mindless, he thought to himself, *just what I need.* Three lagers later, he was laying on the couch staring glass-eyed at the TV. He'd lost himself in thought over the useless log back at the workshop, trying to figure out a way to work around it, trying to figure out how to somehow make it worth the effort he'd already put into it.

Reminds me of my own work sometimes.

There it was, the voice he thought he'd left behind at the lake, the one he thought he could run away from.

"Dammit," Finn sighed. He turned the TV up louder and tried to reassure himself, "It's just the beer talking."

You were wrong, you know.

Finn crossed his arms and focused on the TV. "I should really stop drinking," he said.

She does need you.

"So much for the beer." He flung the remote across the couch and ran his fingers through his hair.

So do I.

"Ha! Ha, ha, ha! You need me? The God of the Universe needs me? That's great. Genius," Finn laughed.

The way you need her, the way she needs you, that's the way I need you. That's the way I love you, but so much greater. Your mind can't even begin to comprehend how deep my love for you is. But right now, Finn, you are rotting from the inside out, just like your log back there. Right now,

you are the obstacle.

Finn was speechless. He had no arguments; he had nothing to throw back in the face of the God of the Universe.

With a groan, Finn stumbled to the bathroom to find his box of sleep aids, swallowed one, and chased it with a swig of beer.

"I assume you'll still be here in the morning," he said to the stucco ceiling as he walked back to his bedroom.

I'm not going anywhere.

He pushed a pile of laundry off his bed, kicked off his shoes, and rolled into his black flannel comforter. The last thing his mind's eye saw as his lids closed was Allaya, laying on the dock while he worked on the shore.

"Finnigan . . ." it was as if she were there next to him.

He dreamed of her all night, in all kinds of situations. They all ended the same. She shut the door on him again and again, all night long, though he could tell by the look on her face that she was fighting the action. She didn't want to shut him out.

Just before the sunlight seeped through the blinds on his bedroom window, he had a more troubling dream. He was in a maze and on every wall there were doors. Each door led down a different hallway, and his mission was to find the one that she was waiting behind. He could hear her calling out to him, getting angry with him. He could feel his heart aching as he searched for her through all types of doors made of all types of wood. Finally, when he felt like he would never find her, he got to a door that looked familiar. It was unfinished. It was ragged. It was rotting. He pushed on the browning spot but it wouldn't budge. The door was stuck, or too heavy, but he knew she was behind it. He could hear her breathing. He could smell her.

"Ally, I'm here. I'm trying," he called to her in his dream. "Finnigan . . ."

He woke with a start, head pounding, forehead beaded in sweat, and suddenly he had a new plan of attack for the rotten log. Perhaps the entire log wasn't ruined. Perhaps all hope was not lost; perhaps he could salvage some of it. Dressing quickly, he grabbed a single slice of bread from the kitchen on his way out the door. He had almost reached the lobby when Tanya turned the corner to come up the stairs, stopping him short.

"Oh, hey," she said, surprised. She was carrying a plastic bag full of things; a familiar-looking sleeve hung out of one of the handles.

Even when standing a step below Finn, Tanya was almost as tall as he was. She was an inch taller on flat ground; her slender, curvy figure had been what had attracted him to her in the first place. She had long, strawberry blonde hair, carefully curled in waves down her back. She was pretty, and dark eye makeup dramatized her eyes in such a fashion that made every guy she passed do a double take. Finn saw none of that now.

"I didn't think you'd be back yet. I was just going to leave this for you next door at Jake's since I already left my key. I was doing laundry and found some of your things at my place so . . ." She held the bag out awkwardly toward him, obviously trying not to be any closer to him than necessary.

"Oh, thanks."

"So, you're back then?"

"Yeah, got back last night." He grabbed the bag from her outstretched hand.

"How was the lake?"

"Um . . . it was . . . good and bad, I suppose."

"Well, since you're back if you want to—"

"Tanya, nothing has changed." He didn't let her finish her thought. He didn't have the patience for her at that moment.

"I know, I know. You made your point. I was just going to say that we could hang out sometime if you wanted. We can still be friends, right?"

No. Not ever in a million years.

Finn didn't want to explore any kind of relationship with Tanya, but he wasn't about to leave yet another destruction in his wake.

"Yeah. Sure. I'll call you sometime," he lied. "Look, I've gotta run. I've got a project I'm working on. Thanks for bringing this by." He waved the bag and jogged down the steps past her.

"So you'll call me?" she called after him.

"Sure thing!" he called without looking back. As he made his way to his truck, his inner battle started again.

See now, why can't you just be with Tanya? She's beautiful and fun . . . annoying and clingy. He groaned quietly. *But she's got her stuff together, sort of. No baggage really, besides those daddy issues . . . maybe we do make a good pair.*

Finn was merely toying with himself, trying to forget about the storm Allaya had started inside him. All he had to do was recall one kiss and Tanya would be but a distant memory. There was just no way she could compare to Allaya, and all the greatest things about Tanya paled in comparison to Ally's laugh, her smile. Together those things could completely change his mood in a matter of seconds. There was so much more depth where Ally was concerned.

I'm the difference.

Finn laughed as he stepped up into the truck, slamming the door beside him. If there was anything Tanya was not, it was religious.

"I'll give you that one! But that doesn't change the way things are right now." He replayed his idiotic comments to Allaya in his mind and slammed his hand into his steering wheel again.

His mother's words echoed in his head: Give him a chance.

Finn was silent for most of the day as he worked at the shop. He quieted his thoughts and focused hard on the project in front of him. The rot had started in the very center near the top of the tree, most likely initiated from a lightning strike, and recurring rainstorms probably caused the residual damage. Most of the top two pieces were useless, but the bottom two could be saved. He began scraping at the rotten center. He had no defined purpose except to prove a point: The log was salvageable.

Back at Herron Lake, Audrey and Allaya sat together on the back porch of the cabin, filling in the gaps of the cross with the rocks they'd collected.

"Ally, Dad is going to absolutely love this. I absolutely love it!"

"And Shara?"

"Definitely. Shara will love it."

"Finn said that they still talk. He said that she's changed a lot."

Audrey set down the glue brush. "She really has. I don't know what it was that had her so bottled up before, but she is like a new person. She is considerate and caring and so much more sensitive now. She misses you, honey."

"Yeah, that's what Finn said," Ally sighed. "One step at a time, Mom."

Audrey patted Allaya's knee and then picked up the glue brush again. "You know, I think that this is a little too big to put inside a frame. We'd have to get something specially made, and, well, I just don't think that's the way to go," Audrey said thoughtfully.

"What are you thinking?" Allaya asked.

"I'm not sure. We could just hang it on the wall as it is, that would work."

"But then it just becomes another cross on a wall. I want it to be set apart somehow. It's got a story to tell, you know?"

"Hmmm. Well, you'll figure it out. Whatever you decide will be perfect, sweetheart!"

Finn wiped the sweat from his forehead, stood back and stared at the one log, hollowed out like a carcass and rid of the disease that would have consumed the entire thing eventually. He still had no vision for what he was making, but he toiled over the wood anyway. He folded his arms and looked around the shop at the three unfinished projects waiting for him. He realized that even with the extensions he'd gotten from clients, he was running out of time to finish them. They were the projects that paid the bills. Deciding that his side project would have to take a backseat, he moved the logs off the workbench and exchanged them with the sofa table that Mr. Francis, a faithful client, was waiting on.

"Time to get on with life," he sighed and started sanding.

Audrey hoisted her suitcase into the trunk of her car and turned to her daughter. "You sure you'll be okay?"

"Mom, my plan was to be here alone anyway. I'll head out in the morning. I'll be fine."

"All right. Will you call me when you get in? Will you come over this week?" She then bit her tongue. "I'm sorry, honey. One step at a time, I know. I'm sorry."

"Mom!" Allaya grabbed her mom and hugged her hard. "That is a step that I need to take!"

Audrey held her daughter tightly and heaved a huge sigh. "I'm so glad to have you back, Laya," she whispered through tears. "I couldn't handle losing two of my babies!"

"Oh, Mom!" Allaya sniffled; the effect that her isolation had on her family suddenly became so clear to her.

Watching her mother drive away from the cabin, Allaya crossed her arms tightly around herself. It was her last night at the lake. The next day she would have to drive the five hours back to Portland and get her mind back in the game—the game of teaching third graders, the game of being a real live person again with friends and family and love . . . maybe. According to her mother, time would tell. But for the time being, she still had one more night before any of that happened, and she was going to finish what she came there to do.

Fifteen

With her Bible, journal, and pen close by, Allaya lay on her back on the floor of the living room, staring up at the ceiling, and began to pray.

"Lord, if there is anything left that you need to take care of in my heart, I am here and I am willing. No more reluctance, no more demands, just openness and willingness." A simple peace began to wash over her as she sang along to an old worship album that played on her iPod in the background. She felt bathed in comfort and affirmed that, as it related to her grief over losing her sister, she was now in recovery. She turned over onto her stomach and stared at the same blank page of her journal that she'd been staring at for the past two years. She bit the side of her lip and picked up the pen.

Dear Marielle,

I can't even begin to explain how this feels. To have to go on and live life without you. I feel like I've been in an emotional coma since we found out about what happened in Sudan. I have missed you so much. I have ached for a way to fill the hole that you left inside my heart. I kept hoping that it would change—that the pain would go away on its own—but I know now that I will always miss you. You will always be gone, and I will always hate that. But I think you'd be happy to know that that hole in my heart isn't going to paralyze me anymore. I'm sorry that I let it go on for so long. I didn't know how bad it was; I didn't know what it was doing to our family. I would do anything to have you back, but I'm sure, since now you've had a taste of what real life is like, you'd never come back here. That kind of makes me smile. It helps me to know that you are so much better off and that the Father is smiling at you, face-to-face. Someday we'll be together again, and though it probably won't matter to either of us then, I like to imagine filling you in on all the details that you've missed over the past few years and on the ones that are ahead.

    I think you'd be amazed—well, if you were still here you would be—to know that Finn Meyers and I have, well, that there's something between us. I don't know what it is or what it will be, but I can't help but think it wouldn't have happened if I hadn't come up here this week. Huh. I just thought of that. Not that I'm going to give your death credit. No way. If I could choose to bring you back, I would give up anything. But God had a plan in all of this and I don't understand it, but I know now that I don't have to. I know that he took care of you, that he rescued you, and that he's rescuing me, too. I wish things had been different, that he had rescued each of us differently so that we could *be together right now, but this is the way it is, and I'm finally accepting it. I will ache for you forever; you were the best friend I ever had . . . will ever have. I miss you, Ray-Ray, but I'm fine now. I'm going to be okay, and I know that, most importantly, you are safe and sound.*

I love you,

Laya

The words flowed across the page, finally filling up the empty lines like paint on a fresh canvas. The page no longer stared up at her as a reminder of the emptiness inside her, but as she turned the page to finish the letter and sign her name, she felt her spirit take a giant step forward. She really believed it; she was going to be okay. A teardrop blurred the ink where her name was written and she took a deep breath.

"That's done," she whispered, wiping at her eyes. But there was still another matter at hand. "Oh, Lord." She sighed and sat up, hugging her knees. Resting her cheek on one knee, she let Finn's face cross her mind.

"Lord, I don't have a clue how this happened. I really don't. This hit me like a tornado! One minute, nothing, and the next? A complete whirlwind of feelings and emotions. What am I supposed to do with this? How am I supposed to respond? And now I don't think we're even speaking! Maybe it's better that way. But I want to talk to him! I miss him and it's only been two days. And we only spent three together! This is insane! What is going on?" Almost immediately she felt her skin begin to prickle the way it did when something big was going on between herself and the Father.

I'm working on it, Love.

But what does that mean? she asked in her mind.

It means that I am at work in him.

This is nuts. It all happened so fast! The things I feel when I'm with him . . . I can't even begin to sort through it all!

I created you in a way to feel and experience certain things, and when they are explored in my timing, I breathe life into them—into you. I know the plans I have for you, and I am working to bring them into fruition.

"What am I supposed to do now?" she cried out loud.

Be.

"Be? As in, the letter 'B'? A bumblebee? Can you just speak normally to me? I need answers here!"

Be at home. Be at work. Be with your family.

"Be," she said the word as if trying it on for size. "I want to be with Finn!"

She meant it. She really did want to be with him. She had begun falling in love with him, and then, well, then he had helped unveil the true colors of her heart and she'd finally been able to break through two years of pain and hiding. But Finn didn't know that. He probably thought she was still mad at him, that he had done the unforgivable. That's why he hadn't called, hadn't stopped by. There was no way he could know how she really felt and what was really going on. She started to get up to get the phone and call his cell, but then she second-guessed herself. Would that be interfering with some greater plan? God had told her simply to "be." She wasn't certain what that meant in regards to Finn, but God hadn't told her to call Finn. Would he have if she were supposed to? She groaned out loud. She was tired of fighting and second-guessing.

"Screw it," she said and walked toward the kitchen. With the phone in her hand, she stared at the post-it note he'd left on the fridge with his number scrawled across it. Anticipation built within her just at the thought of hearing his voice. She bit her lip and carefully dialed the number.

"Hi there, you've reached Finn Meyers Carpentry..."

"Crap!" she said as the message started. She couldn't hang up and call back in hopes that he'd answer the second time. That would be too obvious and her number would show up on his missed calls, but she couldn't just hang up without leaving a message, either.

"... leave a message after the beep and I'll get back to ya!"

Allaya drew in a sharp breath.

Beeeeeep.

Exhale. "Hey Finnigan, it's Ally. I just wanted too, uh, well, I think we should talk. Yeah, I'd like to talk to you. I'm leaving tomorrow morning for home, so, I don't know if you're still here, or if you left, or what, but here's my cell..." She left him her number and clicked the talk button on the phone.

"There. Now I can 'be,'" she said to herself and placed the phone back in its cradle. She had to at least give him some sort of inclination that she didn't despise him for the things he'd said. She'd given him the reins. If he cared like he claimed to, he would call her back.

Finn had the radio cranked up in the workshop and he missed the sound of his phone ringing. He was painting on the last coat of varnish on the sofa table; he'd been working nonstop to finish it. Carefully eyeing over the entire project looking for flaws or drips, he deemed it perfect. He stepped back and let out a huge breath as if he'd been holding it the whole time he had been working. He wiped sweat from his hands and face and picked up his phone. He clicked the button to skip the missed call log and pulled up Corey Francis's number.

"Hi there, Mr. Francis. It's Finn Meyers . . . Yep, it's done! I just gave her the last coat of varnish, and she should be ready to go in a few hours . . . What's that? Oh, it looks great. I think it's going to go great with your new living room . . . No problem! Of course! All right, I'll see you in a bit." He clicked the phone off and tossed it back onto the counter, totally forgetting about his missed call.

It was early when Allaya decided to start her trip back to Portland. She had no reason to stay, and the five-hour drive was long and lonely. Better to get it done rather than to drag out the inevitable. She favored her injured ankle as she lugged her suitcase down the cabin steps, threw it into the back seat of her Civic, and walked back to the house. She braced herself against the walls as she took one last walk around the cabin, making sure all the doors and windows were locked, the fridge was cleaned out and anything perishable had been taken to the dumpster. She locked the door and then took one last journey to the dock, the bucket of leftover stones swinging from her hand.

Allaya stood on the very edge of the dock and let the surrounding beauty overtake her once more.

"I wish I didn't have to leave you," she said to the tiny ripples of lake water. She stretched her arms out on either side of her and turned her face to the sun. "But I won't wait so long to come back again."

She picked up the bucket and pulled one stone out, passing it between her fingers. It was white with black flecks in it, one of her favorite kinds. She tossed it softly into the water and whispered, "Goodbye, Marielle."

Kneeling down on the jagged wood, she slowly tipped the contents of the bucket into the water, watching as the rocks sank out of sight as they reached the bottom.

With a deep breath, she got up and walked back up the dock to solid ground, knowing that she would be able to return home and rebuild her life. She was done wallowing, done being wounded. She might grieve for a lifetime, but she could now live and grieve at the same time. Without hesitation, she got in her car and drove away.

She passed through the small town of Herron Lake on her way back home and pulled into the dirt lot of the small grocery store that Finn's mother owned. Even if he wasn't there, seeing Carolyn would be worth the stop.

The store sign said "Open" when she pulled up, even though it was before nine. Allaya walked in and quickly saw Mrs. Meyers stocking canned goods at the back of the store.

"Just a minute!" Carolyn sang. Allaya leaned back against the cash counter and glanced around the store. It was as though everywhere she went held a little piece of her childhood. She smiled as she remembered coming here with her sisters and her dad to get gummy bears and sour candies during the summer when they were little. She smoothed her hand along the wooden counter behind her.

I bet this is Finn's, she thought to herself, admiring the craftsmanship. A lump rose in her throat.

"All right. Sorry about that. I was just—" Carolyn stopped short when she looked up from wiping her hands. "Ally!" she whispered.

She ran to the girl and threw her arms around her. Allaya didn't hesitate to embrace the woman who had been like an aunt to her for so many years.

"Hi," Allaya said into Carolyn's hair.

"Oh goodness. I don't know why I'm so emotional. I knew you were here. I knew you'd come see me. But, oh, how wonderful it is to see you," Carolyn sniffled. "With color in your face and life in your eyes. Oh, Ally." She put her hand on her chest. "My heart is full!" she said, wiping her eyes.

"Well, of course I came to see you! There is no way I could leave without stopping by."

"Leave? Oh, I guess you're on your way out, aren't you?" Ally nodded.

"Hmmm. Well, can you sit and chat just for a minute? I have coffee made," Carolyn offered.

"Coffee sounds great!"

Carolyn smiled, took Allaya's hand and led her back to the residence.

"What about the store?" Allaya asked.

"Oh, I'm never usually open this early. I don't know why I am today; no one will come before ten!" the older woman chuckled.

"I guess I'm lucky I caught you, then!" Allaya said.

"Hmmm, I guess so!" Carolyn tilted her head thoughtfully as she bustled over to the coffee pot and motioned for Allaya to sit at the table. "So? How was your time here?" Carolyn brought two mugs over and pushed the sugar and cream toward Allaya.

"Well, it was a roller coaster," she sighed.

Carolyn's eyes smiled at her with love and urged her to continue.

"There was just a lot that needed dealing with, as you know, and, well, at the very least, I think I did what I came here to do." She swirled sugar into her coffee, choosing her words somewhat cautiously.

"The very least? Honey, if you did what you came here to do, then, wouldn't that be more than satisfactory? I think it's wonderful. Amazing. Phenomenal!" She threw her arms wide.

Allaya smiled, remembering how Carolyn gushed when she was emotional. She wasn't sure that the woman was privy to the complications that had risen between herself and Finn, so Allaya broached the topic warily.

"Well, there were some . . . er, well, no, there was a distraction . . ." she trailed off, eyeing Carolyn's expression.

The older woman nodded knowingly. "I'm partially aware, and I don't want to pry, but sweetheart, if you want to talk about it, you can. I know how to listen without bias. I won't take sides."

Allaya chuckled; there was no need to beat around the bush with Mrs. Meyers.

"I don't really know what to say, honestly. There was just this burst of emotions and feelings all around me, and maybe I just sucked him into it, or maybe I was drawn to him. Maybe it was all a
mistake . . . but no, I don't really believe that. Oh, I don't know. I guess right now I feel like, since I got what I wanted in coming here, like I need to focus on that and not be greedy and not take

on more than I can handle, you know?" Even as she said the words, she wasn't sure how she would get Finn out of her head or her heart, or even if she was supposed to, for that matter.

"I do know what you mean, and I understand. I know Finn told you about how he came to be up here at the same time as you, so you and I both know that the Father has some kind of greater plan in the works, though none of us can understand it just yet. I think it's wise for you to focus on getting past all that you've been through and to be thankful for where you are. Good things come to those who wait *and* trust!" she grabbed Allaya's hand and squeezed it affectionately.

"But let me say this dear," she went on, "Finn is as stubborn as his father was, and whatever it is that he is battling with our Heavenly Father about right now, it is something he's held on to for a long time. It won't be easy for him to recognize his need. At the same time, when he loves something or someone, Ally, nothing will get in his way."

Allaya was taken aback. She hadn't realized that Finn was fighting an inner struggle as well. She figured him to be somewhat ignorant toward God. Suddenly things began to make better sense.

She cleared her throat. "Is he gone?"

Carolyn nodded sadly, "Yes, honey. He left the night that you two argued."

"Oh," Allaya whispered and looked away, breathing deeply and squeezing her eyes tight.

"Oh honey, I'm sorry. But I just know that there is purpose here!" Carolyn scooted around the table closer to Allaya, putting an arm around her. "He is my son, but I know he's not perfect. I've never seen him so tormented before. He's never been so open with me about a relationship before. He loves you."

"After just three days?" Allaya was almost too scared to believe it.

"Oh honey, when the heart sees what it wants, time means nothing!" she soothed.

"But how come this never happened before? I mean, how many summers did we spend together with absolutely nothing between us? And now, like a tidal wave, we are both completely floored by feelings? I don't get it!"

"Well, for starters, Ally, there was never nothing between you two. You've been close friends almost your entire lives! That's the best place to start something like this. And as for why it's happening now? You just never know. But it has happened now, and it has happened now for a reason."

"My mom said that now I just have to sit back and wait."

"It's true. It's frustrating, but it's true," Carolyn nodded. "I know that the Lord is working on Finn. I also know that until you are both ready, it won't work. For now, Finn still isn't ready to take you on, not because of you but because of your faith, your convictions, your priorities."

Allaya sipped her coffee and sat silently. After a minute Carolyn turned her chair to face Allaya and put her hands around Allaya's face.

"Know this, Allaya Sheldon. The Father loves you, and he has brought you here for such a time as this. And my son? Allaya, my son loves you. I know it in the core of my being. He holds everyone at arm's length so that when there is any sign of retreat or pain, he can just shake that person off and not be affected. But he ran from you, Ally—"

"Yeah, that's a great sign," Allaya snorted.

Carolyn laughed. "I know it sounds bad, but, for him, it means that you got to him deeply. It means that you have the ability to hurt him and he can't handle that. That's how I know that he loves you."

Allaya sat back and let the insight sink in. She supposed it made sense, but she had no way of knowing that it was, indeed, his nature to run. She'd have to take Carolyn's word for it.

"Okay," she said firmly. "Fine. So now I have to wait."

"Praying wouldn't hurt either, dear," Carolyn said quietly.

"So I wait and I pray. I can do that." Allaya sounded like she was planning an attack.

"Just one thing honey," Carolyn said, her eyes narrowed in question. Allaya looked up from her last sip of coffee.

"You do love him?"

The question surprised Allaya. She sat up straight in her chair as if uncomfortable and her eyes grew wide as though caught in headlights. She took a huge breath and was about to go into an explanation of her feelings, but immediately she felt her face get hot and her eyes begin to well up with tears. She looked up at the ceiling, trying to blink them away then looked back at Carolyn and simply nodded her head emphatically while biting her lips together. She wiped furiously at her cheeks, and this time, Carolyn stood, pulling Allaya to her feet to hug her.

"I know, I know, sweetie. Love stinks. But the payoff is amazing. I promise. I promise, he's on his way."

Allaya nodded and pulled away, wiping her eyes again and sniffling loudly. "I'm sorry," she half sobbed, half whispered.

"No, no! None of that. There are no apologies to be made. I remember this time, this feeling. I remember how horrible the pain is of loving someone who's not there to love."

"It sucks."

"It does! It definitely does. But like I said, he is on his way. He loves you, and he'll get to you one way or another."

"I will wait, and I will pray, because I love him too." Allaya squeezed her eyes tight to stop the tears.

Carolyn packed Allaya some snacks and sent her on her way, watching from the store entrance as the car disappeared down the highway.

"Oh Lord," she prayed. "Whatever you've got for those two, please let it come quickly! This stuff is so hard!" She turned on her heel to get back to the canned vegetables that needed stacking, continuing to pray silently.

Allaya prayed most of the way home, as well, but she still checked her phone constantly to make sure she hadn't somehow missed its ring. No calls. She wished desperately that she didn't have to wait. She wished that he would just call her or that she could call him again without seeming desperate. But she knew that she would be interfering then for sure. She'd been given clear instruction: Wait. Be. And she planned to try really hard to do so.

Sixteen

Finn didn't miss another call for days; therefore, he had no new voicemail alerts. It wasn't until a full week had passed when he was in the shower and missed his mother's call that the voicemail icon showed up again. As he toweled off his hair, he listened to his mother's message:

"Just checking in, honey. I hope you're okay. I miss you and I'd love to chat when you have a minute. Love you. Bye."

He hit "seven" to erase the message, and as he was about to punch the button to end the call, he heard the computerized voice say, "Next unheard message."

Huh? He pulled the phone back to his ear again, wondering whose call he had missed and when. He heard Allaya's voice. He formed a fist around the towel he was holding, and his heart nearly beat out of his chest.

Heading home tomorrow? He quickly thought of the date and couldn't make sense of any of it. Then it dawned on him. After he'd listened to the entire message, he pushed the button to get the date and time information. She'd called last Friday before she had headed home on Saturday.

He swore under his breath and threw his phone down on the countertop.

Calm down. Just call her now! he thought.

Then he said out loud, "I can't call her now! She probably thinks I'm a complete ass!"

He cursed again, battling within himself over what to do next. He paced around his apartment a few times and picked up the phone to listen to her voice again and write down her number.

He sat on the couch with the phone in his hand and her number on the coffee table in front of him, trying to convince himself to dial her number.

"What if this is for the best?" he asked the empty room. "Maybe I just need to leave her alone."

And what? Be miserable forever? He continued to struggle in thought and out loud.

"Oh, please. She's not the only girl in the world."

She's the only one I want.

She's the one I want you to have.

His head flung up. He'd managed to silence that voice for a few days, but there it was again. He groaned and tossed the phone on the table, flopping back onto the couch.

"Go away!" he yelled. Then he quieted himself, realizing that by now his neighbors probably thought he had problems because he talked to himself all the time. He rolled his eyes.

You do have problems, he scolded himself.

Remember that old rotten wood?

In fact, Finn had forgotten it. A stack of materials lay on

top of it, and he'd been busy getting back on schedule with his other work. He hadn't even thought of those pieces.

The longer you leave it, the worse it will get.

There was still one piece of wood that needed rot scraped out of it.

That goes for you, too.

Finn got up, walked to his bedroom so as not to be heard by his neighbors, and shut the door, pulling the blinds shut and the black curtains closed over them. The darkness of the room mirrored his mood.

"Fine," he said. "You want to do this? Let's do this." He sat on the black comforter on his bed and looked up at his reflection in the mirror on top of his dresser as the voice prodded him on.

This is about your dad. You and your dad.

"No, this is about you and my dad," he said into the mirror. "He honored you. He respected you. He gave you what you asked for. And you let him die."

Choices have consequences. Your father made some bad decisions, and his illness was the result.

"I know that. But you could have done something! Just like with Marielle. You could have stopped it. You could have stopped her from going! You could have stopped him from his first cigarette!"

That would be interfering with the free will that I gave them, Finnigan. They made choices. Let me be clear with you. You are not going to get the answers that you want to hear today. You will not hear me say that I made a mistake, that I should have done this or that. Hear me say, son, that in light of all the darkness in the world, in light of

all the pain you suffer, and in light of all the pain everyone else suffers, I am still holy. I am good. I gave man the choice to follow me or not. To be this or to be that. It's your responsibility to choose. I won't take that gift away from you, but you have to be aware that the choices you make result in something, whether good or bad. There is cause and there is effect. But in spite of all that, son, I am. I love. I give.

Finn laid back on his bed, totally surprised at the pounding in his chest from the response he'd been given. As firm as Finn was in his stand against God, God was seemingly just as firm in his stand for Finn.

"I just don't get it," he relented.

I asked Marielle to go to Africa. She chose to obey. I asked your father to make sacrifices, as well— some he chose to make and others he didn't. You need not try to understand how it all works, son, you just need to trust that it does. My ways are not your ways, nor are my thoughts your thoughts. But there will come a day when understanding will be yours and you will see the greater picture, the way I see things, and then you will know all that I know. If you choose me.

"I don't think I'm there yet. I'm still pretty pissed off at you."

I know. That doesn't scare me, though. I'm not offended by your anger or your questions. I've chosen you and I know the longings of your heart—all of them—and I want you to have those longings fulfilled.

"What longings?" Finn scoffed.

To be known. To be valued. To feel the pride of a

father, the love of a father. Acknowledgement. Security. To be loved so desperately that your life depends on it.

Finn's eyes grew wide as things he hadn't even acknowledged as truth began to take shape inside his heart. The dark corners had been exposed and secrets had been conjured up from wounds and years that were so far in the past he could hardly recall them.

But there was that very evident void where his father should have been. Even before Steven Meyers had died the void had existed. A big, huge emptiness. It wasn't that he had been absent or abusive; he had been awkward and unavailable. While Finn had begun going through the rights of passage into manhood, his father had been consumed with battling cancer, unable to talk him through the process of puberty or to talk him off the many proverbial ledges Finn had faced as a teenager. He wasn't available to talk about the reason why kissing Shara had held zero satisfaction for him in spite of the way that the evolution of her body over the school year had caused his own body to react upon seeing her that summer. Or about the shameful dreams that would wake him in the middle of the night. Those were the things he'd needed help navigating through. And when Finn had needed an example to look to, all he could see was a man suffering from the consequences of years of bad habits. At the very least, Finn had never touched a cigarette. That was the only positive he'd ever been able to take away from his father's death.

"So yeah. I'm well aware of my issues," he sighed, returning his thoughts to the present and covering his eyes with his hands.

I can fill your void, Finn. I will not go back and undo

what has been done, but I can change things now, and I can make things new. Your earthly father loved you, but he was incapable of loving you the way you needed to be loved and that goes back into his own history and involves things that he lived through as a child. But I can break that cycle. I know how to love you, Finn. I created you. I know what it is that you need.

"You want to be my Father."

I am your Father. I am.

"I dunno, God. I just don't know." He felt his chest constricting.

Do you know that I love you? Above all else?

"No," he sighed and lay back on the bed, staring up at the ceiling, watching the fan whir above him.

I would love to show you that it's true. Will you let me?

"What do you mean?"

Close your eyes.

In one final attempt at defiance, Finn held his eyes open as long as he could, following the blades of the fan in circles until his eyes began to water and he had to blink. He expected to blink and flash his eyes back open again, but the minute he closed them, they felt as though they'd been cemented shut. He couldn't open them, and immediately he realized he had no desire to. This love that was being spoken over him—while something he never would have said he needed—began to lure his heart out of the shadows of his soul. Images began to flash through his mind. He saw clips from different Bible movies that his mom had made him watch as a child, he saw a cartoon reenactment of Jesus' life and crucifixion, and then he saw his mother standing in the driveway as he drove off to Seattle, leaving home officially for the first time, all of his belongings in the back of his truck.

"Oh, Lord, please go with him. Please watch over my baby!" he heard her whisper as tears streamed down her face.

Then he saw his father's face laughing, and Finn realized it was the memory of their first fishing excursion on the lake. His first catch—a tiny rainbow trout, not more than a few inches long—had conjured a pride in his father that Finn had never experienced before. The loud bellow of his father's excited laugh had echoed around the lake, and Finn remembered the absolute joy he had felt in that moment, in being the cause for a smile on that surly old man's face.

Laying on his bed, Finn was unaware of the tears slipping down the sides of his cheeks onto his comforter.

He remembered the evening he had been in a bad accident in a friend's car and that he had walked away from the crash with only a few scrapes and bruises, though he could have been crushed as the car had been.

His father came back into the picture again—in bed, sick and silent. This time Finn saw himself sitting beside the bed in a creaky old rocking chair that used to sit unused in the corner of his parent's bedroom. Finn saw that his own face was turned down and that he was staring at his hands, confused, uncomfortable and scared. He remembered the day. The day before his father died.

Then he saw his father's hand reach out toward him, slow and shaky. Frail fingers touched lightly on Finn's arm. The unexpected touch had startled Finn. His father kept reaching until Finn gave him his hand. Steven Meyers, having lost the use of his voice because of the cancer, squeezed his son's hand with as much strength as he could muster. He looked desperately into the eyes of his son, trying to communicate.

At the time, Finn had been confused and thought the cancer had eaten away at his father's mind as well. He had wondered if his father even knew whose hand he was squeezing. There were tears in the older man's eyes and he pursed his lips together fiercely. His intensity had scared Finn momentarily, and then the man released him and fell back into a deep sleep, one that lasted through the night and then stretched on into eternity as the sun rose into the sky the next day. Now, as Finn remembered the look on his father's face, that desperate attempt to convey something important, he knew.

He was trying to tell me he loved me. Even in his last days he couldn't say it. Oh, God. The thoughts burned into his mind.

The image in his mind turned blinding white, and his hands, both of them, felt like they were being gripped and squeezed just like back in his parents' bedroom with his father. He felt the all-seeing eyes staring at him desperately, but this time he heard the words he had needed to hear so many years ago.

You are my son, and I love you so much—so much more than words or actions could ever say.

It wasn't the first time the Father had spoken this to him, but it was the first time Finn had really heard it. His hands covered his eyes and he began to sob. He turned slowly on the bed, facedown, fists clenched around the fabric of his blanket, tears drenching through to his sheets. The intensity of that love made his heart race and he struggled to breathe. It was painful to let go of the indifference with which he had regarded the Lord. It was painful because as long as he was ignorant, he didn't need to acknowledge his own guilt, his own actions. But now the heavy burden of his choices weighed on him, and he couldn't believe that the Father would take the time to speak such love to such an unworthy man as himself.

But I don't see those things when I look at you, son. I see your struggle. I see who I have created you to be; I've just been waiting for you to get here. Waiting for you to open the door just enough to show you this love. You don't have to live under guilt and shame, Finn. Give all of that to me, and let me renew my Spirit inside of you.

Finn curled his legs into his chest, hugging them in the fetal position. He was afraid to do what the voice in his heart beckoned him to do. He was terrified of being abandoned or let down, or worse, of being a disappointment and thus worthy of being abandoned or let down.

I will not leave you. I will never turn my back on you.

"You're not going anywhere?" He surprised himself by truly begging the question.

Exactly. I am here regardless of your choices. I am always here.

Finn sat up and ran his fingers through his hair. He was exhausted and his face was sticky from tears. He was thankful that he lived alone and didn't have to face anyone else that day.

Deep breath in, deep breath out. He had no other cognitive thoughts. He needed some time. Time to process and sift through all that had been opened up in his heart. Finn was never one to stick around for the hard times; the will to fight had never been his. The urgency he felt was different this time, but he still battled the same thought process he always had: *I don't need this. I'm okay on my own. I'm outta here.*

Allaya's face shot through his mind. He knew if he held

out too long, he would lose her. A different kind of voice than the one he'd been hearing tried to convince him that she wouldn't have him anyway, that she'd already moved on, and that he didn't deserve her.

You're not doing this for her.

That voice silenced the other accusing one.

Let her go.

What do you mean? he thought.

If you're going to follow me and let me love you, you have to let her go. Let me have her.

You mean—

I mean that she is not the reason I want you. And she can't be the reason that you want me.

He wanted her almost more than anything.

Do I have to do this right now? I don't think I can—

I'm here. I'll be here. I'm not going anywhere.

The knot in Finn's stomach was proof enough that something significant was going on. Her voicemail played over in his head and he was angry at himself for missing it. If he'd answered her call maybe they'd be together already.

No. He knew they wouldn't be. He knew for the first time ever, that there was a plan behind all of this, some kind of divine highway, and he was standing right in front of a fork in the road.

Seventeen

After a month at home and back at work, Allaya felt as though she were settling back into the normal life she knew before tragedy had incapacitated her. She felt healthy and balanced even though she still spent many nights laying awake for hours, replaying moments from her time with Finn and stirring the passion in her heart. She'd assumed that with time the feelings and memories might all fade. She wondered if perhaps there hadn't been any greater purpose and if it had all happened just for the sake of happening. But then there would be a nagging in her spirit to pray, and she would pray at length. And then doubt would slip away and she'd find herself remembering Finn again and hoping for the future.

    Reality took its toll, however. There had been no calls, no texts, and no emails. Shara hadn't heard from him, either. Allaya knew that much from her mother who had promised not to share any of the story with anyone. Allaya wasn't ready to field the questions and teasing that would arise if anyone else knew. She made a conscious effort to put him out of her mind, and at the same time she remembered to pray for him as often as she allowed a thought of him to reside in her heart.

She was thankful for the distraction of her own family's reunion. It wasn't that she hadn't seen any of them since the funeral; she had been around them, but she had felt like she was looking at them through a storefront window. Her family responded in stride, tiptoeing around her and making superficial small talk when she was around. Because of her discomfort, she had eventually found excuses for getting out of any kind of family gathering. She had avoided them like the plague. But all of that was over now.

Allaya pulled her car into her parents' driveway and sat there for a minute staring at the small white house with the green shutters where she had grown up. She remembered fights over curling irons and mirror time; Shara had always hogged both. Allaya wondered if they had done anything with Marielle's room. Part of her hoped that they had and another part of her feared that all traces of her sister would have been packed away. She took a deep breath and got out of the car. Her parent's sedan was the only one in the driveway. Shara was still on her way.

That's better. One at a time. She opened the door slowly, the smell of her mother's pot roast filling her senses.

"It's me," she called out and shut the door behind her.

Her father, Terrence, came rushing around the corner and wrapped her in his arms in his signature bear hug, but he didn't let go like he would have normally. He just held her. She could feel him shaking with tears.

"Daddy," she whispered through tears of her own. "Daddy, I'm so sorry."

"I know," he cried, and he squeezed her tighter.

"I just, I didn't know who I was without her. I miss her so much, Dad!" Allaya leaned into her father's embrace, and, for the first time in years, she let him hold her and support her.

"I know, baby girl."

The door opened behind them and a sharp breath drew their attention. Shara had slipped silently through the front door and now held a hand over her mouth, holding back her own sobs.

Terrence reached out a hand and drew her into the embrace.

When Audrey emerged from the kitchen to announce that dinner was ready, the scene at the front door surprised her. She sighed and returned to put the roast back in the oven on a lower temperature.

"You can cook just a little bit longer," she said to the pot, and went to join her family.

"She was part of all of us. We all had to work to find our way back to each other, to ourselves," Terrence said as they began to unwind from each other. He smoothed Allaya's hair with his hand and kissed her forehead. Shara mopped her eyes with the tissue that Audrey was passing around.

"Laya, I've missed you," Shara cried. "I felt like I lost both of my sisters."

"I'm so sorry, Shara." Allaya reached for her sister's hand.

"You don't have to go through any of this alone anymore, Laya. We need you, and you need us," Terrence said firmly.

"I know that now, Daddy. I'm not going anywhere," she whispered, and as she said it, she remembered hearing those words so many times at the lake just weeks earlier. She took a deep breath and wiped her eyes.

The night was spent discovering a new kind of normal for the Sheldon family. They laughed and cried and then laughed some more. Allaya was just thankful to be able to give herself back to her family again, and there was so much comfort and peace even as they were all suffering. Now they were healing together, and that made a huge difference.

After dinner, when Allaya was getting ready to head home for the night, she paused and asked the question that had been bothering her all night.

"Mom? Have you . . . Marielle's room . . . is it . . .?" she cringed, unable to finish her sentence.

"It's the same," Audrey said quietly.

"What are you going to do with it?"

Audrey breathed in and out loudly. "I haven't been able to bring myself to do anything with it," she shook her head.

"Maybe we could help you clean it?" Shara offered with a nervous glance at her sister.

Allaya pursed her lips together and blinked back tears. She nodded slowly, "I think that would be good."

"Okay," Audrey nodded in agreement, "All right."

The next Saturday, the three of them gathered at the house again, armed with boxes and trash bags.

Shara waved her iPod at the other two. "I figured we'd need a good playlist to distract us."

Allaya smiled. The one thing she and Shara had in common was a love for great music. "Good idea," she answered.

"Alright." Audrey took both of the girl's hands as they

stood in front of Marielle's room. "Let's do this."

Neither of them said a word as they walked into the room. It still depicted the life of a college-aged girl. A bulletin board with photographs of the family and of her best friends hung over the top of a disorganized desk. Marielle's packing list for Sudan lay on top of a pile of papers, her messy handwriting filled the page and every item had a line through it. Allaya touched it gently, as though it would turn to dust if she mishandled it.

In the corner behind the white daybed with the purple flowered duvet, sat a large hiking backpack, still full of the last personal possessions Marielle had ever touched.

Audrey quickly stepped over to it.

"I don't want to unpack this yet," she said.

Shara nodded in understanding. "What about the posters and everything? Do you want it all down, or . . ."

Audrey closed her eyes tight and took a moment to collect herself. "There's no sense keeping it up, is there?"

Allaya put an arm around her mother. "Not if we're really going to move on."

Audrey exhaled and said, "Then let's take it all down. Ask me before you throw anything away, and, of course, you can have anything you want, just . . . don't throw anything away until I see it."

"We'll make a throw away pile and you can go through it later?" Shara suggested.

Audrey nodded.

They set to work, taking pins out of posters of handsome actors and grungy boy bands, laying them in a pile on the floor. Allaya was surprised at how therapeutic it felt to clean out the room. With each item she packed into a box she felt as though pressure were being lifted from her lungs; it was easier to breathe.

When the walls were bare, apart from the curtains on the window and the empty bulletin board, Allaya went to work on Marielle's desk while Shara concentrated on the closet. Audrey excused herself to make some lunch, and the girls were left alone in the room.

"I was jealous of you two, you know," Shara said as she pulled a sweater out of the closet and began folding.

Allaya stopped sorting the papers on the desk and turned to Shara. "Because we were so close?"

"Because you were alike, because you were close, and because you knew how to have fun. I was the smart one. I was the one who followed the rules. You two," she got a funny smile on her face, "you two knew how to have fun and not get in trouble!"

"We got in plenty of trouble!" Allaya grinned.

"But not enough," Shara pointed out.

"Yeah, that's true. But we never meant to exclude you from any of that."

"I just didn't fit in. I was the odd one out between the three of us."

Allaya frowned as she considered her sister's words.

"I want to be your friend, Allaya. I've always wanted that. I wanted to be hers too. I wanted us all to be close. It just never happened that way."

"I'm sorry, Shara. I didn't know how much it bothered you. We both always thought you were better than us. We thought that you looked down on us because you were older and more mature."

Shara scoffed. "Do you think it was fun being the mature one? I've always just had this—this feeling of responsibility hanging over my head. I couldn't ever let loose like you two because I was too afraid of the consequences. But you both got away with so much garbage. The one time I ever did anything worth getting in trouble for, Dad scarred me for life! I was so terrified he'd show up if I ever even thought about kissing a boy again! And let me tell you, that kiss wasn't even worth the reaming we got!"

Allaya blushed and pursed her lips together at the thought of how Finn's kissing skills must have improved since those days.

"I wish she were here. I think it would have been easier for us as adults," Allaya said quietly.

"Well, we'll never know now," Shara sighed and went back to her task.

Allaya sat on the stool at the desk and, pushing the various receipts and papers filled with information on the Sudanese people aside, dumped out the contents of one of the drawers onto the desk.

"Oh, jackpot," she whispered holding up a four by five snapshot.

"What?" Shara set down a pair of jeans and peered over Allaya's shoulder.

"Oh my word! Let me see that!" Shara snatched the photograph out of Allaya's hands and nudged her aside to share the stool.

The picture was taken at the lake; it was the three sisters and Finn. Arm in arm on the dock, with infectious grins on their faces.

"Do you remember when this was taken?" Shara asked.

Allaya shook her head. "It could have been a hundred different times. But look, I got that bathing suit in the seventh grade. I remember because Becca Wilson had the same one, but she looked fat in hers."

Shara looked disapprovingly at her sister.

"What? It was the seventh grade! And she did look fat!" Allaya laughed.

Shara shook her head. "So it was before Mr. Meyers died, then, and before that awful kiss."

"Was it really that bad?" Allaya took the picture back and studied the younger versions of herself, her sisters, and the man that she now loved.

"Um . . . yes. It was horrible," Shara rolled her eyes.

"Horrible? Really?" Allaya was curious.

"Yes. Besides the fact that everyone knew about it, it was definitely the worst kiss ever. We pretty much collided with each other's lips. I think I even had a bruise!" she laughed.

"Huh. That's interesting," Allaya said with a chuckle.

"Why?" Shara cocked her head to the side.

"Well, I think it's safe to say that he's learned a few things since then." Allaya, blushing, eyed her sister carefully, watching for her response.

"Huh? What do you mean?"

She blushed again and raised her eyebrows at Shara, biting her lip.

"No. Way." Shara sat back and crossed her arms. "No way!" Her jaw dropped.

Allaya took a deep breath and grimaced. "He was at the lake while I was there."

"Shut. Up. Tell me everything!"

Allaya recounted her short visit to the lake and the details surrounding her relationship with Finn. It was hard to talk about it like it was in the past, especially when Shara asked questions like, So what do you think will happen? and, Have you talked to him?

Allaya wanted to let go of it, to move on, but there was no relief in sight. As she relived those moments for Shara, she felt all of the intensity of them all over again. When she ended the story with her last attempt to reach Finn, Shara sat back again and pondered.

"I don't know, Laya," she shook her head. "He hasn't even tried to contact you?"

"Nope," Allaya shrugged.

"This all happened while you were at the lake?"

"Three days."

"Dang."

"I know."

"Well, here's what I know about Finn. He loves us—all of us—and he would never do anything to hurt us. He's not a jerk; he could never be. I think you should just—"

"If you tell me to wait and pray, I might have to slap you," Allaya interrupted, giving Shara a dark look, to which Shara snapped her mouth shut and looked away.

"Crap," Allaya said as she propped her elbows on the desk and dropped her head into her hands.

Hours later, Marielle's belongings were packed or thrown away and each of the girls had at least two boxes and a few bags full of things they wanted to keep.

Audrey sighed as she looked around the room, which was now void of personality other than the duvet and curtains. Boxes were stacked neatly along the wall under the window waiting to be moved to a new home—the attic most likely—until enough years had passed that Audrey could willingly let go of a little more.

"I have dreaded this day for so long," Audrey sniffed.

Allaya slipped her arm around her mother's waist and rested her head on the woman's shoulder.

"Promise me you'll never go to Africa," Audrey whispered, pulling Allaya into an embrace.

"No worries there, Mom." Allaya shuddered at the thought.

In Seattle, Finn had taken up the rotten logs again. He'd begun on the second piece, scraping all the rotten parts out. It hadn't come out as clean as the first one. He'd had to work much harder to save the second half, and as he struggled with his project, he found himself challenged also with the Father who was relentless in his pursuit.

You are my son, God would say. Conversation had become natural between them. Finn no longer fought it, but he found peace in the process. He found that the more he engaged the Father, the more he wanted to hear, to know, to learn. And he learned that the more he listened and learned, the more understanding he received. He was becoming more at peace with himself.

There was still the matter of his pent up anger in regards to his father's death, though, and how he'd conditioned himself to keep anyone who tried to get near him at a distance. The facts were that Finn's father had failed him. The truth was that Steven Meyers had had his own demons that Finn knew nothing about.

There had to be reasons for the way his father had acted. As Finn's eyes were opened to seeing details more clearly, he realized that the way he'd been trying to protect himself mirrored the way his father had responded to him. That was a huge awakening for Finn. He imagined one day having a son of his own, and what it would look like for that child to grow up with the same kind of father that Finn had had.

    As he saw the potential of the cycle repeating itself, Finn threw himself to his knees. He allowed the walls to be dismantled, and he found himself chasing down the love that had been promised to him through so many visions and moments of clarity in the weeks that had followed his heart-rending afternoon with the Father in his bedroom.

    His thoughts were still often consumed with Allaya. At one point he would have sought her as his prize—his reward for a job well done—but he was beginning to understand that the real reward was the relationship between Father and son. It was something he'd never experienced before, and she had been the catalyst that had brought Finn to the place he was in now. If things worked out and she became an even more integral part of his life, then it was a reward they would get to share in together. He never even considered the role he had played in her life.

    He had had moments where he felt the impulse to call her. He had even come close a few times, but for some reason, he always chickened out. He felt like too much time had passed since missing her call. What would he say? He felt like a fool for not being more attentive a month ago. In those moments, though, the Father would remind Finn that Finn released her and that whatever was going to happen to them was now in the

Father's hands. The peace that followed after those reminders fueled his patience as he waited for the right time to reach out to Allaya again.

November came quickly. Leaves changed colors, and the air turned crisp as fall took over the skies. Finn sat at his workshop, staring at his two hollow log halves. He was at a loss. He'd saved the wood, gotten rid of the rotten parts, and he still had no idea what was to become of them. He sighed loudly, sitting in exactly the same spot he'd been for days.

"Why can't I just move on? Why can't I just forget about these stupid pieces of wood? There is better lumber out there!" He berated himself. But no matter how hard he tried he couldn't rid himself of the need to create beauty from the ruins.

For where your treasure is, there your heart will be also.

"Huh?" Finn cocked his head to the side as he replayed the words. His mother had quoted that verse hundreds of times when he was growing up. He said the words slowly and out loud as he looked at the logs.

"For where your treasure is . . ." and then his eyes widened. "Yes! That's it! Yes!" He jumped up, and immediately he knew exactly what to do. It would be tricky to make it work, to achieve his standard of quality, but he had never turned down a challenge, and this one would be well worth the effort.

Allaya was particularly tormented as she lay in bed that night. She could not for the life of her get the sleep she needed to relieve her of the fire in her stomach. If she closed her eyes, she could feel his lips and smell his cologne. Only three days worth of memories, but they were so vivid in her mind! Thankful that the next day was Saturday and she could sleep in, at around two a.m. she finally got up to get a glass of milk.

She sat at her kitchen table and prayed: "God, seriously, this is really getting old. I've been praying, I've been waiting, and I've heard absolutely nothing from him! I don't know what you want from me. It's pretty obvious that this isn't happening. So what? Am I just supposed to sit here and wait for him some more? It's been three months! I can't keep going like this. It hurts. I don't want to hold on to this anymore. I don't want to do this anymore."

I have good gifts for you.

"I know, you've said that . . . a few times! But, if it were him, wouldn't this waiting period be over by now? Can't you give me other good gifts?"

My timing is perfect, Laya. You will see.

"I just don't know, Lord. I don't want to waste any more time."

My time is never wasted.

"Okay. But please hear my heart, Lord. I am tired, and I want this resolved. I need to move on if this isn't happening."

When it's time, you will know. I promise.

She gulped down her milk and went back to bed, with the knowledge that giving Finn up and moving on would be require a lot more than a nod from the heavens.

Stores had begun playing holiday music weeks before Thanksgiving came around. Lights were up around the city and turkeys were on sale for twenty-nine cents a pound. Finn had finished his project and had never felt more proud of something he'd created. It had taken more hours than anything he'd ever worked on, and that said a lot, considering the simple-looking shape and design. No one would ever know how complicated it had been to make that one rotten tree into the masterpiece he had in front of him. He carefully loaded the finished product into the back of his truck and covered it with a mover's blanket, securing it in some padding so it wouldn't slide around. It was one piece he could not fix if something were to happen to it, and if something happened to it, well, his whole plan would be compromised.

Nothing is going to happen, he told himself. He picked up his phone and made one last phone call before setting out on his journey.

"Hi, honey," Carolyn chirped on the other end of the line.

"Hey, Mom."

"Are you heading out?"

"Yes," he said, exhaling slowly.

"All right. I love you, and I'm so proud of you. I just know that this is going to be amazing."

"Thanks, Mom. I love you, too. Will you, uh, will you pray? About all this?"

She chuckled, "Honey, I've been praying about this for months. It's going to be great."

"Thanks, Mom, for all that you've been to me, my whole life . . ."

"Oh nonsense. Don't start that now! Go get her honey and give the Sheldons my love!"

"All right. I'll talk to you later."

"I'll be waiting!"

"Bye." Finn tucked the phone into his pocket, opened the door to his truck and took another deep breath. "Here goes nothing." He climbed in, started the ignition and headed toward the Interstate.

Eighteen

Allaya took her time getting ready to head to her parents' house for Thanksgiving dinner. She styled her hair and applied her makeup carefully. It was a special occasion, equal parts happy and sad. It was their first holiday all together, though they were still missing one member. They usually ate the big meal on Monday while everyone was off work, but her parents had planned a get-together with some friends from church and they'd moved their family dinner to Saturday instead. The cross memorial sat on Allaya's table, wrapped in bubble wrap. She had waited until she felt a significant urge to reveal it to her family, and, for some reason, Thanksgiving dinner was going to be the occasion.

They all knew she had something to share with them, but only her mother knew what it was. Allaya had held out long enough—things had settled into a new ebb and flow for her family and their emotions were sturdy enough—that it was time to give a physical memorial to Marielle's life. She had a tombstone at the cemetery where she was buried, but this was one they would have within reach and it was a reminder that her sacrifice was not in vain. Allaya's only regret was that she hadn't figured out a way to enclose the cross. Her mother was right: it would have been too awkward to encase it in some sort of frame. It wasn't symmetrical and some of the branches bent in odd directions. It was perfectly imperfect. But it wasn't enough of an issue for her to hold out any longer. Besides, she hoped that her dad would be able to come up with a solution.

Allaya wrapped a scarf around her neck, threw her coat over her arm and raised the cross onto her shoulder. She rolled her eyes and snickered as the words to the old song "Take Up Your Cross" came to mind. She left her apartment, locking the door behind her.

Allaya could smell the turkey before she even opened the door. She paused and took a deep breath, hoisting the cross onto her knee one last time. It was her first family holiday since Marielle died. When she opened the door with her free hand, all the rest of the Thanksgiving dinner smells came gushing out at her. She blinked back tears as she felt her heart fill.

I've missed this so much! she thought as she stepped inside.

"Laya? That you?" her mother called out.

"Yep, I'm here!"

"In the kitchen!"

She maneuvered herself through the door and set the cross behind the couch immediately in front of her. The room hadn't changed in the fifteen years her family had called this place home. Just like at the cabin, everything had stayed the same. Her mother's old flowered couches that were once her pride and joy for years had taken verbal abuse from the girls at every family meal, holiday and special occasion.

"It may be ugly," Audrey would retort, "but you can't get quality like this anymore!"

The rest of the house was just as dated, which meant that nowadays the decorating was actually back in style—almost. Allaya ran a finger over the crushed velvet orange flowers, and, for the first time ever, she appreciated the fact that things hadn't changed in the house. When she had finally returned to her own apartment after the funeral, she'd wanted to destroy everything in it, but she had only gone so far as to take pictures off the walls, especially the family ones.

"Honey?" Audrey came from the swinging door drying her hands on her apron, "You okay?"

"Yeah, I'm fine. Just admiring your furniture," she winked.

"Oh, brother. Quit that and come help me!" Audrey rolled her eyes in a huff.

Allaya dropped her purse and coat on the couch and followed behind her mother into the kitchen.

"It smells great in here!" Allaya exclaimed.

"It should! I've been working all day! It seemed like things would never get done. Everything was against me. The turkey didn't defrost quickly enough, so that set everything back. I burned the first batch of pies, so, we'll only have two to choose from—"

Allaya gasped in mockery, "Only two pies? For four people? What will we do?"

"That'll be enough out of you, young lady. Come stir this gravy!" Audrey handed her daughter the spoon and motioned toward the stove.

"Where are Dad and Shara?"

"Your father went to get more butter at the store, and Shara should be here any minute."

As though she knew they were talking about her, they heard the front door crash open and Shara crying out, "A little help, please?"

Audrey ran out to oblige her while Allaya kept stirring the gravy, waiting for it to thicken up.

"You cooked?" Allaya asked incredulously as Shara pushed through the kitchen door with her arms full and followed by her mother.

"Yes!" Shara defended. "Well, no, not really. The rolls are store-bought, but I did warm them, and the salad, well," she sighed. "No, I didn't cook." She set the rolls on the table.

"Well, I think we're almost ready!" Audrey said, bending into the oven to check the turkey. "If your father would just show up now!"

The girls bustled around each other getting the rest of the food on the table. It looked and smelled like it could have come out of a *Martha Stewart Living* magazine.

"It looks beautiful, Mom," Allaya smiled.

"Seriously, we should take a picture and send it to a magazine!" Shara pulled out her phone and opened the camera app.

"Oh, you two. If only you both had gotten my talent!" Audrey teased.

"I can cook!" Allaya put her hands on her hips. "I'm a good cook!"

"Sure, if you want to eat spaghetti forever," Shara grinned.

"Well, it just so happens that I do want to eat spaghetti

forever!"

"No way. Not tonight. Tonight, my darlings, we feast!" Audrey imitated and Italian accent and threw her hands out over the table, as if displaying her work.

"Fantastic!" Terrence's voice boomed from behind them. "I'm starved and this looks a-maz-ing!"

"Now that it's all *finally* done, nothing can stop us from enjoying!" Audrey motioned for everyone to take their seats at the round table.

Before her father sat down, Shara kicked Allaya under the table and mouthed, "Any news?" as she did every time they saw each other. Allaya was beginning to wish she had not said anything to Shara about Finn. Yes, Shara had changed a lot, but she was still Shara.

Allaya furrowed her eyebrows as if to say, "Not here, not now!" and shook her head.

Shara shrugged apologetically.

Terrence sat down and grabbed Shara and Allaya's hands and bowed his head. The girls each took one of Audrey's outstretched hands and bowed their heads as well.

"Father," Terrence's voice filled the room, "we have an abundance of things to be thankful for tonight. Not the least of these is the family that you have surrounded us with and those you have brought into our lives as we have needed extra support. We thank you for the work you have done in all of us—bringing us each back, in your time, to the place that you have us today. We don't understand all the things that you do, Lord, but we trust in your perfect will, and we know that you know what is best. Thank you for my girls, Lord, all of them. We pray that you would bless this food, and this family, in your mighty name.

Amen."

A chorus of amen's flowed around the table, which were, in turn, followed by a "Dig in!" from Audrey. She hadn't ever been so pleased to have provided a meal for her family. Marielle was gone and she would never return to them on this earth, but Allaya was back and that was cause for joy. Audrey's happiness shone in her eyes as she served her family.

Just as Allaya poured gravy over her potatoes and turkey, the doorbell rang. Everyone looked up at each other, puzzled.

"Did you invite someone else?" Terrence asked his wife.

"Does it look like I invited someone else?" she glanced around the table clearly set for four, with the ever-present empty fifth chair at Terrence's side.

"Girls?"

They each shook their heads.

Audrey sighed, "Whoever it is, is going to pay dearly for cutting into this dinner!"

She stood up, tossed her napkin down on the chair and stalked out, letting the kitchen door swing behind her. Allaya tried to catch a glimpse of who it was as the door swung slower and slower until it stopped moving. They could hear the front door open. Voices were muffled, but there was definitely no "paying dearly" going on.

Soon Audrey came back through the door, and, eyeing Allaya, she said, "Terrence, Shara, let's go," and she hustled them up from their chairs.

"Audrey! What in the—" Terrence looked at his wife as if she'd gone mad.

"Terrence. I said, let's go. Shara, come on," Audrey said firmly, stomping her foot.

"Mom! We're just about to eat! Why doesn't Laya have to come?"

"I said, let's go!" She gave each of them the look that indicated she meant business. The swinging door opened and Allaya felt as though her heart jumped right out of her chest and onto the floor. She dropped her fork and knife and caught a sob in her throat.

"Well, I'll be! Finn Meyers! What a surprise!" Terrence bellowed, pushing back his chair and standing up. He stuffed his hand into Finn's hand and pulled him in for a hug.

"Uh, hi, Mr. Sheldon," Finn smiled nervously. He was taken aback and stumbled into the older man's embrace. "I'm sorry to interrupt—"

"Terrence. Now." Audrey raised her eyebrows and jerked her head to the door.

"Audrey, I don't know what's gotten into you! We haven't seen Finn in ages! What in the devil—" and suddenly, his hands dropped to his sides. He looked back at Allaya, who had not yet recovered. Her jaw was still hanging open and she looked as if she weren't breathing. Shara quickly grabbed her dad's arm, and, with Audrey's help, they guided him out of the kitchen and out the front door. He protested all the way.

"Ally," Finn started.

A sob burst through her lips. He stepped forward slowly, wringing his hands together.

"Ally." He was breathless. "I had this whole thing prepared in my head. I practiced it all the way here from Seattle . . ."

Her mouth was still gaping open; she was an incoherent mess of emotions. As he searched for words, she had to fight to hold back tears.

"I know it's been way too long, and the last time we saw each other I was horrible to you—"

She put up her hand to stop him, but she was shuddering, totally overcome. She had no tears yet, but she also had no words.

"No, please, Allaya, let me talk first, and then you can say whatever you want." He walked over to her and grabbed her raised hand.

His hand on hers was like a match on gasoline. She thought for sure her hand would ignite as he touched it.

"I am so sorry for the things that I said to you at the lake. I had no idea what I was talking about, and I know that I hurt you, and I would do anything to take back those words."

She stood up and pulled her hand away, pressing it against her chest, trying to breathe.

He was afraid she was livid with him and that she would kick him out. He forced himself to push forward before she could do just that. "Please, can we sit? Can I tell you some things?"

With a panicked nod, she left the kitchen and went to sit on her mother's ugly sofa. She squeezed her hands between her knees and stared at him, still not speaking.

Finn sat gently beside her, searching for words. "I really had this whole thing prepared. Just a second," he said, as he closed his eyes and tried to concentrate, "I . . . I need to thank you."

She stared up at him in surprise.

"Thank you for being my friend. Thank you for caring about me, but most importantly, thank you for shutting me down and for walking away from me."

Allaya let out another sob, and she quickly clamped her hand over her mouth.

"You have no idea what God has done in my life because of you," he shook his head. "No idea."

He grabbed her hand from her mouth and pulled it into his lap.

"Ally, I never knew what it was like to have a father who loved me; I always felt like I was just a detail in my own dad's life. Then when he died, I just shut my heart down. I believed that the only chance I had to have a father was gone. I blamed God for the cancer, I blamed God for not healing my dad, I blamed my mom for not taking a stand against my dad's habits, and I told myself that if they had truly loved me, they would have sacrificed everything for me."

Allaya tried to speak again, but Finn kept going.

"But God showed me some things about my dad and about my dad's life, and he showed me some reasons why my dad was the way he was with me. He reminded me of some times in my childhood when my father really did show how he felt about me. My father loved me!" A smile crossed his face. "And even if he hadn't loved me, I've experienced a new kind of love. I know now that God is my real Father, that he doesn't fail and that he did sacrifice for me. He's done so much in my life to show me how he feels, and I've just turned away and ignored him. I thought I didn't need that love. But I do, so badly." He paused and took a deep breath.

"And then after all that came to a head, the only thing left in my heart," he reached for her other hand, "was you."

She drew in a staggered breath.

"Allaya, God told me that if I wanted to receive him, that I had to let you go. I had to put you in his hands. So I did."

Allaya's face paled and she looked at him, blinking away scared tears.

"But I didn't give up on you, or us," he added quickly, picking up on her confusion. "I gave you to him. I trusted him with the future, I told him that whatever happened with us was totally going to be in his hands, and I promised I wouldn't do anything until he told me I could."

Allaya stared at him with the same confused and concerned look.

"That's why it's taken me so long to get here. I had to make sure that this was what he wanted and that I wanted him no matter what. You couldn't be the reason. And you're not. He used you in my life to get me to where I needed to be in order to see him for who he really is. So for that, I thank you." He looked deeply into her eyes.

"Finn," she whispered.

"I'm not done. I'm sorry," He smiled apologetically. "I have a gift for you. Hang on."

Jumping up from the couch, Finn disappeared momentarily out the front door.

Allaya sat in complete shock on the couch, paralyzed by his words. Her mind was reeling.

I promised.

Tears streamed down her cheek as she leaned against the couch with her hand over her mouth again. Her stomach was balled up in knots.

"All right," he said, as he reemerged into the living room. He was carrying a huge, awkward, box-shaped packaged that was wrapped in brown paper. His arms stretched around it as he set it down in front of her, and then he sat beside her again.

"Before you open it, I want to say just a few more things. First of all," he looked at her wet cheeks, "Ally, you've got to stop wasting these!" He caught a tear on his finger, just like the first time she cried in front of him. She grabbed his hand and pulled it to her chest, her eyes still full of emotion.

"The thing in this package—that I made for you—is from that tree that I found out at the lake, the one I was working on that day this all started." He sat up and held her hands, looking into her eyes. He went on to explain about the rot that he found and how frustrated it made him. He told her about the dream with the rotting door that he couldn't get beyond, and he told her how the Lord had showed him all the rotten parts of his own life that were standing in the way of his freedom and wholeness.

"I had to work really hard to get all of the rotten pieces out of this log, and then after I did, it left such a mess that I had no idea what I could possibly make from the leftovers. I don't want this to sound ridiculous, but I realized that I was rotting from the inside out just like the wood was. I feel like God used this old tree," he knocked on the package, "to show me how he could fix me. Just like with the log, there was so much work, so much shaving and sculpting, that he had to do in me to get rid of all my rotten parts and piece me back together. It took a long time, and at the end of it I still wasn't sure what we were creating." He reached forward then, letting go of her hands.

"Then one day, in the midst of all the struggle and change I was going through, a verse that my mom used to quote all the time came to my mind. Then I knew exactly what I was supposed to create, and I knew it was going to be for you." He took her hand and guided it to the package.

Allaya looked at him, uncertain.

"Open it," he whispered.

She pulled on the string and slid it off, pulling the paper away to reveal the most beautifully carved treasure box she had ever seen.

She gasped and reached her hand out to trace the words that he'd etched into the wood and stained a darker color than the natural, untouched finish of the rest of the box.

```
"For where your treasure is,
 there your heart will be also."
         Matthew 6:21
```

Natural blemishes showed on the wood, and she could see the details where he'd had to intricately carve pieces so that they fit together to form perfect corners and straight lines. She ran her fingers over the smooth wood and looked back at him.

"It feels like it took forever, but it was so worth all the back-breaking, heart-breaking hours. It got me to this place where I am now. This was what was holding me back from getting to you. I mean, there was obviously more to it than that, but the timing of it all—what I was going through—was so connected with how I maneuvered my way around this piece of wood. There were so many times when I wanted to pitch the whole thing, and I felt the same with my own journey. I felt so helpless sometimes, like it would never end, like I would never finish it. That I would never reach the goal."

Allaya finally found her voice. "Finn, it's the most beautiful thing I've ever seen!" she whispered.

"Wait, Ally, before you say that, open it," he said slowly. "Open the box."

She eyed him curiously but did as he requested. She opened the lid slowly and the scent of pine came pouring out. It reminded her of being at the lake, of being in his arms, the taste of his lips on hers. She closed her eyes and breathed in slowly.

"Ally, please open your eyes," he nudged her.

She opened her eyes and peered into the box. On top of a bed of roses was a little blue box with a white ribbon. Ally threw her hands up to her face in shock and gasped. Finn reached in, grabbed the box, and knelt beside her.

"After everything I've told you—even after all that—I know that I don't deserve you. You are the most amazing woman I have ever known. I don't know how you feel anymore—if you still care about me or not—but even if you don't, I want you to know that I love you, and I want to spend the rest of my life trying to live up to being the kind of man that you deserve." He held the box tightly in his hand, with his other hand holding hers.

"You are my treasure, Allaya."

With both hands he slowly opened the box and took the solitaire diamond ring out. "No one will ever love you like I do, and no one will ever be able to captivate me the way you do. You are my treasure, and you hold my heart in your hands." He took a breath and looked deep into her eyes. "Will you marry me?"

She barely even saw the ring; she could not tear her eyes from his.

"I love you. How could I ever stop?" she said.

That was all he needed to hear. He pulled her to him and kissed her mouth. It was like coming home. The past few months played over in his mind. He felt like he'd been wandering out in the cold, totally lost, and then a light had led him home to the place where he belonged. He felt her body shaking with sobs, but she was kissing him back as though she could not get enough.

He tore his lips from hers to whisper into her hair, "I love you, Allaya Sheldon. I love you more than life."

His tears flowed freely, as they had for the past three months. His life finally meant something to him, and it wasn't just about her. He had found value and purpose—for the first time ever—in simply being the one thing he'd always felt he'd been cheated of being. A son.

"Yes," she whispered.

He pulled away from her and said, "What?"

She grinned a huge grin. "I didn't give you an answer. It's yes, I'll marry you."

All of the months of hard work, emotional turmoil, and spiritual revelation all came pouring down on him and he began to laugh a loud, hearty laugh from the core of his gut. Relief and joy washed over him and he pulled her to his chest, unable to control the sounds coming out of his mouth.

Allaya felt it too, and soon she was laughing along with him, her heart full to bursting.

Good gifts. Because I love you. Good, good gifts.

When they finally collapsed against the couch, breathless from laughing, Finn slowly slid the ring onto her finger. The diamond sparkled up at them.

"Finn, it's so beautiful!" Allaya sighed as she held her hand up to the light to admire it. She sat back against the couch again and pulled him so she could lean against him. "I missed you so much," she said, and she combed her fingers through the sides of his hair. "I was so scared that I'd never see you again."

"I wasn't going to let you go that easily. I loved you, Ally. I just needed to work some things out . . . like you did."

"I know, I know, it just hurt so much in the mean time—being without you. I kept waiting and waiting and begging God for answers!"

"You spent all that time— "

"Waiting for you. I love you, Finnigan, I wasn't complete without you."

He sighed in amazement. This woman who he so admired, who was more than he ever could have asked for, waited for him. Wanted to marry *him*.

I love you. I want the best for you.

Finn and Allaya both nodded in unison, and then stared at each other in surprise.

"This is so overwhelming," she whispered.

"Tell me about it! There I am, minding my own business and then, BAM, my whole life changes the minute I see you again."

She smiled and tucked her head under his chin. They sat in silence, enjoying being with one another with nothing but the old mantle clock ticking in the background and the sound of their own breath. Suddenly, Allaya remembered the cross.

Finn toppled to the ground with a grunt as she pushed him off and jumped off the couch.

"What the—?"

"Finn!! It's perfect!"

He was rubbing his knee where it had hit the coffee table when she'd launched him off of her. "I'm confused," he said in a daze.

She leaned over the edge of the couch and pulled the

cross out. It was still covered in bubble wrap and a blanket. She unwrapped it carefully and held it up for him to see.

"Whoa. Ally, that is amazing. You did a fantastic job!"

"Yeah, but don't you see? It's perfect!" She scooted over to the treasure box, carefully pulled out the roses, and lay the cross at an angle so that it was standing on its side. She tried shutting the lid. "Perfect!" she exclaimed with a hand over her mouth.

"Whoa," Finn crawled over and opened the box to peer in.

"Whoa is right!" She stood up and looked around the room for the perfect spot to display the memorial. "Here, help me, will you?" she began to clear firewood and old newspapers from the side of the fireplace. Finn dragged the box and the cross over to the spot she was clearing, and he adjusted it so the lid would stay open to display the cross.

"Ally, this is incredible."

"I know!" She took his hand. "We make a good team! We always have." She wrapped her arms around his waist and hugged his side. Finn tipped her chin up with one finger and softly kissed her. He would never tire of her lips, of her tight grip on him. To know that she longed for him as much as he longed for her would fuel him for a lifetime.

Tears fell down her cheeks, but she managed to get a hold of the sobs. She suddenly thought of her family, her mother's fantastic dinner that was getting cold on the table. She knew her mother well enough to know that even with all the fuss that had been put into the meal her mom no longer cared about it. Love was more important. Her father, however, was a different story.

Ally peeled herself away from Finn and got up to look

out the window. "I wonder where my family went."

Finn chuckled, "They're sitting in the car just down the street. I saw them when I went out to get this." He tapped the treasure box.

"Come on. Let's go get them. It's Thanksgiving, and we have a lot to be thankful for." Ally held out her hand and together they went to get the rest of her family.

They stepped out on the front stoop and Ally grinned up at him. "I think you'll probably be needing to have a conversation with my dad, too. Right?" she smiled.

Finn let out a breath. "I'm thinking so. I would have done that first, but I didn't know if you would even see me, and, frankly, your dad scares the you-know-what out of me! I didn't want to go through that unless I had to!" he winked.

"It's all part of his plan to scare off the weaklings. Besides, I think he'll be more upset about the fact that his dinner is cold!" She grinned and pulled him off the step toward the direction of the family car.

Apparently, Audrey had filled her husband in on the necessary details in the car. When Ally and Finn approached them, Terrence stepped out, his face pale, but he simply nodded at Finn and gruffly shook his hand, pursing his lips together to hold back the fatherly display of emotion.

When he turned to Allaya, she held up the hand with the engagement ring on it and whispered through tears, "Daddy, can I marry Finn?"

Shara and Audrey, who had climbed out behind Terrence, gasped, and Audrey's hand flew to her mouth.

Terrence laughed and brushed quickly at his eyes. "It just so happens that we have an empty chair at our table, Finn," he said, nodding. "I would be honored if you would fill it."

Allaya threw her arms around her father, and he struggled to keep his composure.

"Come on, everyone! I can heat everything up in the microwave!" Audrey grinned and put her arm around Shara.

Terrence peeled Allaya out of his arms, kissed her on the cheek and then followed his wife back to the house.

Finn and Allaya walked hand in hand back to the house, unable to tear their gaze from each other.

Epilogue

If it had to be winter, the lake in January was the most beautiful place to be. It was completely frozen over, and there was about a foot of snow on the ground the weekend the small family wedding was scheduled. Up until that week, snow had quickly turned to slush and had made the lake properties huge mud pits. But on the Thursday that the Sheldons packed up and drove away from Portland, temperatures dropped and fresh snow covered the ground.

No one had stood in their way when they'd decided to get married as soon as possible. When she'd sensed her father's hesitation, she echoed the words that Carolyn Meyers had spoken to her.

"Daddy, when the heart sees what it wants, time isn't important!" It had silenced him and he'd never attempted to say anything else again. He knew she couldn't do much better than Finn Meyers. He'd always had a feeling about that boy.

Only Finn's mom, his aunt and uncle, and the Sheldons

would be there, so there was no need for a rehearsal. On Friday night, Audrey took the girls for dinner in town. They sat waiting for their drinks to come and Shara grabbed Allaya's hand.

"Are you nervous?" she asked excitedly.

"Nervous? No, but I'm so excited I can barely stand it!" Allaya exclaimed.

"No, I mean, about—" Shara gave her a knowing look and nodded her head.

"Oh Shara!" Audrey exclaimed.

"What! I want to know!"

Allaya snorted, "Um . . . ha . . . Uh, no. I'm not."

"Oh," Shara was surprised and a little disappointed. She had wanted to play into Allaya's fears a little.

Allaya wasn't comfortable sharing the details with her mother, so as Audrey looked around for their server. Allaya shot Shara a look back, one that clearly said, "Drop it." Shara lowered her eyebrows in question, and then all of a sudden understanding flooded her face and her jaw dropped open. Allaya kicked her under the table. Point made.

Shara recovered just in time for her mother to turn back around.

"I know it's going to be cold tomorrow, but it will be absolutely beautiful, Laya!" her mother swooned.

"I know. It's perfect. I love it here so much." Allaya stared dreamily out the window at the snow that was still falling.

Back at the cabin with Allaya and Shara secured in their room, Shara grabbed her sister's hand and pulled her down onto the bed.

"Shut up!" she whispered incredulously.

Allaya rolled her eyes, "Shara—"

"You and Finn had sex?"

"No! Shara! No! Of course not! I mean . . ." she sighed. Painful memories came flooding back. The only person she'd ever told about Matthew was Finn. She'd alluded to him at the lake, and then in the midst of their engagement, they'd had the inevitable conversations about each other's histories. The only other person she'd ever imagined telling had been Marielle. It seemed almost wrong to divulge her secret to Shara, but . . .

Be.

Allaya quickly snapped out of her reverie. She realized that holding back because she hadn't been able to dish to Marielle was the wrong way to react. That was the kind of attitude that nearly destroyed her life for two years. Shara was waiting expectantly.

"It was with Matthew," she answered.

"SHUT UP!" Shara exclaimed again, "When? Is that why he left?"

"What! Shara! No!" she slapped her sister on the arm. "He left because I turned into a zombie!"

"Oh, right. Sorry."

Allaya sighed and dove into the story. She told her sister about the timing of it, about how much she wanted to talk to Marielle about it, about the marriage talk.

"I wish we'd been closer then, Laya," Shara said quietly at the end of the story. "You could have talked to me about it."

"I know, Shar, but we were both different people then. Our priorities were so different. We had no idea about anything! Either of us!"

"I suppose what's important is that we have each other now," Shara sniffed.

"It is important, Shara. You're the only sister I have."

Shara gave her a half smile and hugged her. "I love you, Laya."

"I love you, too, Shar!"

The sun glanced off the snow and made for a bright Saturday morning. Allaya sat on the bottom bunk staring out the window. The day had arrived.

My promises never fail.

She smiled and closed her eyes. "God, you are so faithful. I don't deserve all that you have given me."

But that is why it is so precious. By your standards you don't deserve it, and I am giving it to you regardless of what you think. You are my princess, and I want nothing but the absolute best for you.

She breathed in a huge breath to calm herself. *Today is the day.* The last time she'd spent so much time away from Finn—and this time it had only been two days since she'd seen him—she hadn't known what the future would hold for them. She had wondered then if she would ever see him again.

There was no doubt in her mind that it was what God had planned from day one. Nothing about her life, or the life of anyone in her family, had surprised him. He'd always known that Marielle would choose Africa. He'd always known that she would be attacked. He'd always known that Allaya would collapse inside of herself, and he'd always known that Finn would be the one to pick up the pieces. All she had was longing. Longing for the clock to move faster, past the hours until midday, when she would meet Finn on the dock outside and commit her life to him.

Finn, on the other hand, wasn't nervous; he was anxious.

Come on, come on, come on! he kept repeating in his head. It helped that it wasn't as cold that day as it had been the rest of the week. The snow was sticking, but he knew that if the sun kept shining as brightly as it was through the clouds, the snow would all melt away by the next night.

He stood with his back to the shore, staring out over the frozen lake. He'd never dreamed that his impromptu trip to the lake last summer would result in his own marriage. Before that week, he had figured he probably wouldn't ever get married. But then Ally came along and changed everything. She became like oxygen to him, and he couldn't breathe in deeply enough to be satisfied. He recalled the moment when he surrendered himself to the Father, when he had imagined what kind of father he would be to his own son. Ally had been the one in the vision with him. There could never be anyone that would ever compare to the woman that he had been given. The boards under his feet creaked and he turned to see the women walking up the dock.

"She's ready, honey," Carolyn said as she embraced her son. He let out a huge breath.

"Are you okay?" she asked.

"I've never been better, Mom. Never." He hugged her back and released her. His uncle, who was a minister, stood beside him, waiting for Mr. Sheldon and Allaya to walk toward the dock. Shara and Audrey stood on the other side, gripping bouquets of deep red roses, each grinning with tear-filled eyes.

Terrence took his daughter's hand and walked her down the steps of the cabin. He turned toward her and said, "You are beautiful, honey. Finn is the luckiest man I know, besides myself. I am so proud of who you have become, and all that you have come through." He choked on his words and blinked back tears. "I love you, sweetheart."

"Oh Dad! You're going to make me cry!" Allaya sniffed.

"All right, all right." He took a deep breath. "I'll stop. Are you ready?"

"So ready!" she smiled and squeezed his hand.

Her hair cascaded down her back in full curls, and she wore a simple white gown with a fur shawl over top.

As Finn gazed at his bride while she walked down the dock, he remembered the night of the storm, and he couldn't think of any other words to describe her—she was an angel. He had seen her countless times since that night, but she was still just as beautiful to him as ever. Nothing could detract from her beauty.

It was brisk outside. Everyone was bundled up tight. But the two lovers were warmed with the passion they'd discovered just months ago on that very dock. It was only right that they would join their lives there.

They stared into each other's eyes and committed themselves to serving and loving each other. He put a platinum band on her finger and said, "I'm not going anywhere."

She slid a larger ring onto his finger and echoed, "I'm not going anywhere." Finn's uncle pronounced them man and wife. They kissed. She cried and he laughed. He picked her up and kissed her again.

They spent the evening together celebrating as a family up at the Sheldon's cabin. After a time, Finn began to drop hints to his wife that he had was ready to leave the family behind and concentrate solely on her.

He whispered in her ear, "I have something for you."

Curiosity roused, Allaya kissed her family goodbye and allowed excitement to well up within her. Carolyn handed something to her son and then he winked at Allaya and motioned for her to follow him. He led his new wife outside to his truck, opened the door for her and then walked around to get in on the driver's side.

"Are we going to the hotel now?" she asked in a coy voice.

"Nope!"

"Where are we going then?" she asked, surprised.

"You'll see." He drove all of a three-minute distance from her parent's cabin and pulled up to another cabin down the road. She looked at him questioningly.

"Isn't this the Abbott's cabin?"

"Nope," he grinned.

"Did they sell?"

"Yup."

"Are we renting it?"

"Nope."

"Finnigan Meyers. Tell me right now what's going on," she demanded.

"That lake, those docks, the beach, the forest around us—they all hold so many of our best memories, and I want to keep making memories here with you. Happy Wedding Day, Ally," he said and held out a key to her.

"What?" she gasped and grabbed the key, which had a tag attached to it that read:

Love Mom, and Mom and Dad

"Wha-at?" she blurted, "We have a lake house?"

"Wait till you see inside." He opened his door and darted around the truck to let her out. As soon as she stepped out of the car, he swept her up in his arms and kissed her hard on the mouth.

"I love you, Allaya Meyers," he smiled.

"I love you, Finn Meyers," she said in amazement.

He carried her up the steps and through the front door. A fire was blazing in the fireplace, casting the only light in the room. She could make out a champagne bucket on the floor beside a plush green sofa. Finn deposited her on the sofa and sat close beside her, reaching for the bucket.

"I can't believe this!" she whispered, her hands covering her mouth.

Finn smiled as he poured the champagne into a flute for her.

"Can you believe we're married?" he asked as he poured his own glass and sat back against the sofa.

Allaya let out a small laugh, "If someone had told me back when I was thirteen—"

"I would have hog-tied 'em!" Finn grinned.

She closed her eyes and sat back, imagining their old lives.

"She would have loved this, you know?"

"The cabin?"

"No, us." Ally opened her glistening eyes.

"Do you think this would have happened if it weren't for—" he asked cautiously.

She smiled lovingly at him. "I think this," she motioned between them, "has always been part of the plan. But surviving Marielle's death took me to a place with the Lord, with myself and with you that I don't think we ever would have reached otherwise. Maybe I'm wrong, but if anything good can come out of the past few years, this is definitely it."

Finn reached for her hand. "Are you ready to see the rest of the house?"

"Finn, I've seen the house before—*oh!*" She blushed as realization dawned on her. "Yes, I'm ready to see the rest of the house."

Leaning forward, he kissed her slowly and then pulled her up into his arms and led her down the hallway. Candles burned in the rooms they passed and Allaya bit her lip in anticipation. Finn turned the corner to open the door to the master bedroom.

There were candles lining every piece of flat furniture in the room and rose petals strewn about the floor and bed. It was the only room in the house that had been completely redone. He would tell her later about the painstaking hours he and his mother had spent ripping down woodsy wallpaper and how Shara had spent hours searching online for the perfect bedding. The walls were now complimentary shades of cream and chocolate brown, a large mirror covered one of the walls, and a mahogany dresser stood beneath it. The duvet cover that Shara had finally settled on was cream with brown stitched flowers across it.

Finn set her down and began to remove her shawl. She gasped as she took in the room.

"It's so beautiful! Did you do this?" she asked.

"I did, with help. I wanted tonight to be amazing."

He swept her hair up in his hand and kissed the nape of her neck, creating the desired effect: goose bumps. He chuckled at her and kissed each shoulder before spinning her around and kissing her mouth.

"Tonight was going to be amazing no matter what, Finn,"

she sighed.

"I just can't believe this is real," he sighed as he gazed at her.

"This is as real as it gets. You are my husband," she whispered. "I love you, Finnigan. I love you so much."

"I am all yours," he said. "One hundred percent yours, and I'm not going anywhere.

Acknowledgments

This book was made possible by a crowd of amazing donors who took me at my word and decided that I was worth promoting. Special thanks for their incredible sacrifice and support goes out to Kyle and Amanda Steed, Colin and Cyana Montgomery, Liz Wiggins and Roger and Colleen Ogram. With each of your donations, my jaw dropped in awe, and I was completely overwhelmed by the Father's goodness. Thank you so much! As well, thank you to everyone else who gave and posted about my book/campaign on Facebook, Twitter and anywhere else. I could not have done this without you!

Special thanks to Keith Peeler Photography for donating my author head shots and to Blake Campbell for coming to my rescue in the final hours of this process! You two have blessed me immensely!

Thanks to my friends, Charisse, Kimber, and Dani who were the first to read the book and send their support. To Lona, Olivia and Sherilyn, who saved me hundreds of dollars on "pre-editing." To Laurie, who perfected it and helped me to become a better writer for the future. To Marissa, who helped tie up all the loose ends and Sallie, for challenging me to demand more of myself and reigning me in when I got out of control. To Jessie, for being one of my biggest fans, and one of my dearest friends. To Becky, for friendship that has seen me through some of the darkest times of life and for being the first person to tell me that it's okay to get angry with God. Ben and Robin for all that you have brought into my life from wisdom to family, and for all of your help in the publishing process. To my parents, who have always believed in me and raised me to seek the Father in all things. Finally, Rocky, my husband who believes that I am able to accomplish more than I've ever dreamed of, and is willing to do whatever it takes to see me fulfill this dream. You and the boys are what it's all about. Everything else could disappear, but the love that binds us will always remain. Thank you for this. I love you.

Ultimately, to my Heavenly Father who gave me a gift and then told me I was allowed to use it. This has been one of the greatest surprises you've given me. I am humbled that you would use me to further your kingdom, and I pray that you are able to move with freedom in the lives of women across the globe because of this book.

STONES OF REMEMBRANCE

FOR MORE INFORMATION ABOUT JULIE PRESLEY AND HER UPCOMING PROJECTS, VISIT WWW.JULIEPRESLEY.COM

CPSIA information can be obtained at www.ICGtesting.com
Printed in the USA
LVOW040508171112
307594LV00002B/1/P